Kingpin Killaz 2

**Lock Down Publications and Ca$h
Presents**
Kingpin Killaz 2
A Novel by *Hood Rich*

Kingpin Killaz 2

Lock Down Publications
P.O. Box 870494
Mesquite, Tx 75187

Visit our website @
www.lockdownpublications.com

Lock Down Publications
Like our page on Facebook: Lock Down Publications @
www.facebook.com/lockdownpublications.ldp
Cover design and layout by: **Dynasty Cover Me**
Book interior design by: **Shawn Walker**
Edited by: **Lauren Burton**

Hood Rich

Stay Connected with Us!

Text **LOCKDOWN** to 22828 to stay up-to-date with new releases, sneak peaks, contests and more…

Thank you.

Kingpin Killaz 2

Submission Guideline.

Submit the first three chapters of your completed manuscript to ldpsubmissions@gmail.com, subject line: Your book's title. The manuscript must be in a .doc file and sent as an attachment. Document should be in Times New Roman, double spaced and in size 12 font. Also, provide your synopsis and full contact information. If sending multiple submissions, they must each be in a separate email.

Have a story but no way to send it electronically? You can still submit to LDP/Ca$h Presents. Send in the first three chapters, written or typed, of your completed manuscript to:

LDP: Submissions Dept
Po Box 870494
Mesquite, Tx 75187

DO NOT send original manuscript. Must be a duplicate.

Provide your synopsis and a cover letter containing your full contact information.

Thanks for considering LDP and Ca$h Presents.

Hood Rich

Chapter 1

Heinous

My heart beat rapidly in my chest, pounding so hard I couldn't help but hear it inside my ears. Sweat slid down the side of my face and dropped onto my chest. It felt like everything was moving in slow motion. I watched my best friend and right-hand woman, Brat, jog across the parking lot headed for her Cadillac Escalade truck when two '87 Chevy Caprice classics rolled into the parking lot of the hotel. The car in front had a masked gunman on each side of it. They were sitting on the windowsills, hanging out of the back of the car with automatics in their hands and red rags covering their faces. The passenger of the car stuck a Tech .9 out of the window and lowered his eyes, holding it with two hands, ready to spray.

It was like I could see the entire scene unfolding in my head before it had the chance to. Brat jogged gingerly across the parking lot as if she didn't see our enemies bearing down on us. I had my mother in the back seat of my Explorer. She was trying her best to recover after overdosing only ten minutes ago.

While I struggled to manage that bit of terror, my sister, Leah, was already passed out in the middle of our hotel room's floor. She'd fallen faint, battling complications from a gunshot wound to the abdomen from when she was shot by a bullet meant for me about a month prior. The night of her shooting still haunted my mind every second of every day.

So, I was stuck. I had two women I loved and cared about in the back of my truck hanging on to life by a thread, and I was under attack by one of many enemies. It was the definition of life in Chicago.

My truck vibrated like a phone, hit rapidly by bullets that seem as if they would never stop coming.

I feared the worst for Brat. The last I'd checked, she had been a short distance away from getting into the truck when all the shooting started. Not more than five minutes earlier she'd told me how she'd just lost her mother, brother, and two nieces. All of them had been murdered by our enemies. We had so many of them that we couldn't say for sure who had been the culprit. The only option was to tear the city of Chicago up piece-by-piece.

But, in order to go that route, we'd first have to survive this attack. Our chances were slim. I had less than five bullets left. I didn't know how far that would get me and my Queens, but I was sure I was going to make every last one of them count.

I waited for another pause in the gunfire, sat up, and turned the ignition on my truck, ready to throw it in reverse. One of the Chevys slammed into the back of me so hard my head jerked forward and hit the steering wheel, causing it to beep. My head snapped backward. I could feel a trickle of blood drip from my nose. It ran down my cheek and off my chin before I could wipe it away.

Whoom. Another car slammed into the left side of my truck, smashing the door inward. My mother started to scream at the top of her lungs in pain.

"Jahrome! Jahrome! Baby, my leg! My leg, baby! Help me! Please!"

Boom. Boom. Boom. Boom.
Doom. Doom. Doom. Doom.

Taat! Taat! Taat!

A barrage of bullets shattering every window in the truck, even the rearview mirror. I ducked as low as I could to the ground, the heavy scent of gunpowder in the air. My mother continued to scream at the top of her lungs. That worried me.

"Get that bitch-nigga, Blood. He in the front, behind the steering wheel! Come on!" One of the shooters yelled.

I could hear glass crunching underfoot. I was beginning to panic. The handle of my driver's door was jiggled.

"Open that bitch, Jo. Get that nigga! That's two million dollars for the mob!" I heard.

I reached and pulled the gear shift into reverse, then stepped on the gas with my hand. The truck lurched and shot backward at full speed, slamming into one of the Chevys with a loud *wham!* The crunching and smacking of metal resonated loudly.

My mother began to scream so loud that I knew something was seriously wrong with her. Gunfire erupted once again, shaking my truck.

I pulled down the gear shift, and threw it in drive, jumped behind the wheel and side-swiping one of the Chevys before taking off like a rocket across the parking lot with two cars in heavy pursuit of me, busting as if we were in a cowboy movie or something.

I got out of the parking lot and made a strong right, fishtailing. My truck smashed into a minivan before straightening. I stepped on the gas. "Mama! Mama! What's wrong? Why are you screaming?" I asked, sweating like crazy. I looked over my shoulder at her as one of the Chevys got close and started to shoot again.

"The door! The door, baby! It's stuck on my leg! I can't take this pain. It hurts," she screamed.

I couldn't see exactly what I needed to because we were once again under gunfire, and I was trying to drive the truck to get away from them. I made a strong left onto a side street and stepped on the gas again, then looked over my shoulder to see the Chevy gaining on us.

One gunman sat on the windowsill in the back of the car, busting a Tech. His bullets ricocheted off of the metal of my truck. I continued to step on the gas until I got to the intersection of Ashland. I sped through the yellow light and nearly crashed into a city transit bus. I drove a bit on the curb before gathering myself, rolling back onto the street.

"Mama, listen to me. I need you to be strong. We're almost away. Please, just be strong, and I got you. You hear me?" I looked over my shoulder to see her crying tears of pain. There was a big pool of blood surrounding her body.

Four feet to her left was Leah. She was on the floor, knocked out cold. Her eyelids fluttered. I felt sick to my stomach. What the fuck had I gotten my family into? This was all my fault.

I peeped the scene behind us and saw the Chevy that had been chasing us turn off of the busy street. I gave a sigh of relief and wiped sweat from my brow.

I swallowed my spit and looked over my shoulder at my mother again. She was shaking now, sweat all over her face. Her eyes rolled into the back of her head.

Kingpin Killaz 2

"I can't take this, Jahrome. I can't take it. It's too much." She fell backward and began to seize uncontrollably.

"Mama! Mama! No! Please!" I turned off the busy street and threw the car in park before rushing from my seat, getting ready to kneel beside her, when I heard a car slam on its brakes, then the sound of doors opening.

"Kill that bitch-ass nigga, Blood. Don't let him get away. That's two mill, my nigga!"

My eyes bucked wide open. I rushed back to the driver's seat just as the shots went off in rapid fashion. Before I could even reach the seat, I felt three hard punches in my chest knocking me into the passenger's seat. The pain was so intense that I pissed on myself. It felt like hot charcoal was being held to my chest.

"Finish that nigga, Blood! Kill him! Kill him!" came the commanding voice again.

I struggled to get back to the driver's seat. I felt weak. *Boom.* Another bullet slammed into my right arm. *Boom.* Then my back. Everything went black.

***

The first time my eyes opened, there were two paramedics looking down on me, both white, one a female with big glasses. She had her right hand over her left, giving me CPR while the other paramedic, a white dude with spiky hair, kept telling me to stay with them. To hold on, they were going to get me to the hospital. He held a defibrillator in his hands.

I passed out again.

11

Hood Rich

When I woke up the second time, I felt like I couldn't breathe. My chest hurt, and so did my lungs. There were stinging pains in the backs of my hands, and tubes had been put up my nose and through my airways.

I felt like I was being tortured. The pain was so intense that it was impossible for me to keep my eyes open. I squeezed them tight and passed out again.

I could hear voices all around me, but I couldn't fully make out what they were saying. I could feel them poking and prodding, sticking me in certain places before I was turned this way or that. Then came the slicing. More pain and agony. My eyes threatened to roll backward in my head. I tried to jump off the table, but they held me in place, forcing me to endure even more pain. My mother came across my mind. I yelled out for her. Yelled out for my sister. I needed to know where they were and if they were okay.

There was a sharp pain in my collarbone and my back and chest. The world seemed to spin around me. Bells rang loudly. My throat got tight. It locked up on me, along with my heart. I felt paralyzed, then weak. I tried to scream out for the doctors to help me, but it was too late. I was slipping. Slipping. Falling into a dark abyss. The pains of my body were intensified.

And then, before I could groan in agony and despair, all of the pain stopped and I was free.

***

I stood with my eyes bugged out of my head as I

looked ten feet ahead of me and saw my father sitting in a big, red leather chair, dressed in a white three-piece suit with red Gators on his feet. He had a Dobbs hat on that was tilted so I could not see his eyes from where I stood. Behind him were two eight-foot black beasts. They had red eyes and mouths full of sharp teeth. They seemed to be laughing, saliva dripping down their mouths and blood all over their hands, which were topped with sharp claws. Each beast had a hand on my father's shoulder.

They stared at me as if they knew something I did not. My father motioned to me with his hand. "Come here, son."

I slowly made my way over to him, eyeing the beasts the whole time. Behind the trio was a lake of fire. Inside of the fire were skulls and bones. Loud screams resonated from it. The closer I got to them, the hotter it got. By the time I was standing in front of my father, I was drenched in sweat.

All of a sudden the ground began to disappear until only a small portion was left. Enough for me to stand in front of them and for them to remain on solid ground. The lake of fire surrounded us like an imminent destination. I swallowed as my heart got to beating so hard in my chest that I swore it was going to break out of my rib cage and flee my body before it was too burned.

"So, son, you've finally made it. I knew it wouldn't be long," he hissed and tilted back his Dobbs hat to show me his eyes were as red as the beasts' standing behind him.

"Pop, I thought you were dead, man. I missed you. You should have listened to me. We should have left the Gardens before this stuff took place, man. Damn. Mama doing heroin now. Leah got shot. I think the bullet was meant for me. I'm losing my mind, Dad. Ever since you left, it's like I can't think straight. I been knocking niggas' heads off for you, though. The city gon' bleed red until I avenge your death. That's my vow to you."

My father laughed as the beast on his right began to rub his chest. Suddenly, it turned into a form of a woman. I watched as she transformed into Pesos' baby mother before my eyes. Her razor-sharp teeth were dripping with blood. "You killed me for no reason, Jahrome. Now you're here." She started to laugh. It sounded like she was wheezing after a long cough.

The beast on his left turned into Tommy Kid, another person I'd murdered in revenge of my father. Then the one on the right turned into Lloyd's niece, and then Lloyd himself. Slowly, but surely, the beasts began to turn into all of the people I'd killed or had others kill for me. They were going through transformation after transformation.

All the while my father stayed the same, laughing at the top of his lungs. The skin of his face began to peel. Blood dripped out of his eyes as tears. He looked up at me and nodded his head. "Your mother using is your fault, son. You're the reason she's slowly dying. Or is she dead already?" he asked, frowning at me, then smiling again. "Leah was hurt because of you. All you do is cause everyone else pain. But you don't have to worry about that anymore. You're in hell now, baby. You're going to reap what you've sown." He frowned, mugged me

14

with hatred, and slowly began to stand up.

I took a step back and almost fell into the lake of fire behind me. I could see the souls reaching out for me. Half of their faces were burned off. They were on fire, being tortured in an everlasting lake of lava. I looked down at them, then up to my father. "It ain't all my fault! You should have never took me there. Had you not, you'd still be alive, my mother would not be on drugs, and Leah would have never gotten shot. It's just as much your fault as it is mine!" I was steaming mad, ready to go at my old man. I didn't like him placing my mother and sister's downfalls solely on me. It was unfair. I loved them more than my own life.

He stood all the way up and seemed to tower over me, despite the fact that since the age of sixteen I'd grown more than four inches taller than him. He busted out of his three-piece suit and right before my eyes turned into a bigger version of the beasts standing behind him. His body was all gray and full of muscles and veins, his neck as thick as a tree trunk. He snapped his big teeth at me as blood slid out of his mouth and along his big neck. "Your soul or theirs. Make the decision right now. Choose them or yourself. Do it now." He spoke in a voice that sounded distorted.

The souls in the lake of fire continued to reach for me. Their piercing screams sounded like nails on a chalkboard. I covered my ears. "What are you talking about, Pop? Whose souls?"

The beasts behind him continued to turn into the many people I'd killed over the years, both young and old, men and women, so-called friends and foes.

Hood Rich

The ground below my feet got a little smaller.

My father grew another ten inches taller, balled his hands into fists, and hollered. Big, black wings popped out of his back with veins going through them that pulsed before me. I could tell they were filled with blood.

He pointed at my face with his long nails. "Choose right now. Either your mother and sister's souls to drown here in hell for an eternity, or your own. Tell me right now! I won't say it again."

A pitchfork appeared in his left hand. His once-black skin turned a bright and shiny red with smoke coming from it, his eyes balls of fire like the sun.

"Take my soul, but you leave them alone. I am their sacrifice! You hear me? Take mine, muthafucka!" I rushed him with both of my fists balled, ready to attack and even kill him if I had to.

Before I could get my hands on him, he seemed to vanish into thin air. Then I was falling off a cliff, headed for the lake of fire filled with souls screaming and burning up. They reached up for me, waiting in anticipation of me joining them in their eternal torment. I waved my arms like crazy in the air, hollering at the top of my lungs in fear of the unknown. It got hotter and hotter the closer I got to the lake. My skin began to burn, it felt like the worst pain I'd ever experienced in all of my life, and it was so hot I couldn't breathe. I was choking.

And then I fell into the center of the lake of fire. All of the souls pounced on me at once, biting and ripping pieces of me away from my frame. No matter how much I tried to fight back, they were too strong. They were angry, full of rage and hatred for me having taken their lives or orchestrating the taking of their lives. The pain was unbelievable, more than I could handle.

Finally, I gave up the fight and allowed them to take me out of the game.

Hood Rich

Chapter 2

"Heinous. Heinous. Baby, please wake up. Please. I need you."

I slowly struggled to open my eyelids, which felt like somebody was forcibly trying to keep them closed. The more I opened them, the worse my head pounded.

Yani placed her hand on my face and laid her cheek up against mine. "Baby. Baby. Oh my God, I thought you were going to die. They say you lost so much blood. I don't know what I would do without you." She rubbed my chest and kept her face up against mine.

"My mother, Yani," I said, out of breath. "Where is my mother?"

Yani took a step back and held her hand over her face. She shook her head as tears came down her cheeks. "Baby, she not doing so good. I'm so sorry." She took my hand in hers and rubbed it against her face.

I struggled to sit up. I felt weak and like I was about to throw up at any minute. My torso felt like it was being hollowed out. My back hurt, and there was so much pain coming from below my neck that I didn't know how much longer I could take it. "Yani, what's the matter with her? Where is she?" I asked, wincing in pain as I tried to sit all the way up.

"She's here in the hospital, baby. So is Leah. But your mother is in a coma, and has been for the last three weeks. You were in a coma for two, and you've been fading in and out ever since then. They had to give you a blood transfusion. I've been worried sick,

Jahrome! Damn, you can't keep taking me through this," she screamed and broke down beside my bed all the way to her knees. "I love you too much, but I can't handle this. We need to get the fuck out of Chicago. Everywhere I go it's niggas and females talking about the two million dollar bounty on your head. Everybody is looking for you so they can handle you and cash your life in. We're living on borrowed time, Heinous. We need to leave this city."

Before she could finish crying her heart out to me, the door swung open and slammed back. "Well, well, well. Look who it is," the tall, bald headed detective chimed. He stood well over six feet with dark skin, brown eyes, and a serious face. His goatee was nicely shaped and graying. He went by the name of Detective Taylor. He was the same detective who had come to my hospital room the last time I was shot up and my father was murdered. Back then I hadn't given him the time of day, and I had no plans of giving him any this time, either.

"So, you just gon' barge in my man's room? What's good with that? Ain't nobody call you. We don't need your assistance, neither," Yani snapped. She'd watched her little brother be gunned down by the Chicago Police Department after they'd mistaken him for the wrong person. She hated the police even worse than I did.

Taylor scoffed and curled his upper lip. "Still bitter, huh? Yeah, well, life goes on. I'ma need you to step out of the room while I speak with Jahrome here. If you refuse to do so, I will have you arrested for tampering with a criminal investigation and whatever else I can slap on yo' li'l, pretty ass. I'm sure those roughnecks down at Cook County would thank me later, you know, having a treat such as yourself coming through the doors guaranteed to spend at least 72 hours before you're even seen by a judge because our system is all backed up. So, we can play it however you want to. The ball is in your court," he challenged with a smirk on his face.

Yani stood up with a mug on her face. "I ain't about to let you do nothing to my man. I don't know you, homeboy, and you can watch how you talking to me. I don't care if you are a police."

"Yeah, bruh, quit all that slick talking. That's my Queen right there. She just making sure I'm good. She ain't got nothing to do with what you about to holler at me about." I felt the morphine being pumped into my system. It was making me drowsy. I wanted to go in on this pig for coming at my woman sideways, but it was hard to muster the strength and words to do so.

"Yeah, well, if I were you, I'd tell her to go and wait in the waiting room, because if she don't, I'm going to make her a part of the investigation. And if that happens, she's going to have to come down to the station every other day. How y'all wanna play it?" he asked, pulled out his eight-inch tablet.

I reached out for Yani. She came over and laid her head on my chest. "Baby, it's good. Just go chill out there and let me holler at twelve right quick. It shouldn't take long. Why don't you go check on Leah and my mother for me? Can you do that?" I asked, slurring my speech a li'l bit. I was starting to have double vision. The room was spinning just a bit.

She stood up and looked angrily across the room

at Taylor. "What if his punk-ass try something with you when I ain't in here. Then what? You already know how they get down."

"He ain't on shit, baby. Trust me, I can handle my own. Now, g'on out there and chill for a minute. Make sure my people straight. That's an order, Boo." I patted her on her big booty to get her going. The movement caused my collarbone to scream in pain.

Yani kissed my cheek. "A'right then, I'll go check on them. But you betta not try nothing with my man, Taylor. I'm hip to y'all bullshit. Y'all already took my brother."

Taylor held the door to the room open for her. "I assure you if I wanted to do anything to him, you wouldn't be able to stop it. Now, go. Come back in a half an hour or so."

She walked past him and looked him up and down. "I don't know who you think you're fucking with, but my man definitely ain't about to talk to you for no half hour. What you think this is?"

He laughed and slammed the door in her face. "We'll see about that, li'l girl." He activated his tablet and stepped beside my bed, tapping on the screen on of his device.

"You ain't have to slam the door in her face, nigga. That shit ain't cool." I situated my body so most of my weight was on my right side. My back, shoulder and collarbone were killing me. I needed them to up the morphine dosage.

He waved me off. "You got a lot of explaining to do. I got bodies dropping all around this city because of you, and I don't like it one bit," he spat with saliva flying from his mouth.

Kingpin Killaz 2

"I don't know who you been talking too, but that shit ain't got nothing to do with me. As you can see, they hit up me, my mother, and my sister. How can I possibly be responsible for bodies dropping all around this city? I'm in a fucking hospital bed!"

He shook his head. "Look, we ain't gon' play that game, li'l nigga. I know what's good. I got CIs all around this city, and every time we receive a call where there are more than three people killed at one time, upon further investigation it's found out that their murders lead back to the beef between you and Pesos. You've gotten King Lloyd's gang in the middle of this, and from what I'm being told, even Lost Boy's Bloods are tangled up in this bloody mess. Word on the street is they have a two million dollar bounty on your head. They want you dead or alive. How you feel about that?" he asked with a smile on his face.

I laughed. "Well, I hope ain't nobody been paid just yet, because as you can see, I'm still alive and muthafucking breathing."

"Eight times. You've been shot eight times within the last three months. It's amazing that you're still breathing. Yet you lay there like it's a fucking game, you stupid, black son of a bitch."

"Man, fuck you!" I hollered. A pain shot up from my collar bone all the way down my spine. I closed my eyes and groaned. I was all screwed up.

"Oh, it's 'fuck me,' huh? Well, what can you tell me about these people?" He held his tablet out in front of me and showed me a picture of Lloyd alive, and then how I guessed they'd found him all cut up and in a bloody mess. Then he showed me a picture of Pesos' baby mother alive, and then her after-death picture. She lay on the carpet with multiple bullet holes to her face and body. He went on and on showing me pictures of people I'd killed, and even some I didn't. It didn't make me feel no type of way. I felt absolutely nothing. In my opinion, they were murdered because I had to. It was a part of life.

I shrugged my shoulders. "I don't know none of them. Why are you showing me these pics? I thought I was the victim here?"

He broke out laughing, bent over, coughing and everything. It must have gone on for a full two minutes before he pulled a handkerchief out of his inside coat pocket, dabbing at his eyes with it. He shook his head, still hunched over. "Boy, now that was the funniest shit I've heard all week. I needed that. Whew, you're a riot." He stood up and replaced the handkerchief. "Not only are you a riot, but you're a fucking cold-blooded killer, and I want yo' ass for what you've done to my city." He frowned his ugly face. "Now, tell me what you know about the murders of the people I've shown you." He held the tablet in my face again, swiping through the pictures.

"Look, bruh, you can show me this shit a million times, I don't know none of them. And I don't give a fuck about none of them. I got my own issues. Have you shown their families pictures of me and mine?" I asked, wincing in pain. My collarbone felt like it was being crushed. I needed a nurse, a doctor, or something. I couldn't believe they had not been in to check on me since I'd woken up. That seemed very unprofessional to me.

Taylor nodded his head. "Okay, so you wanna

play these games then, huh?" He replaced his tablet and leaned into my face. I could smell the scent of musk with a hint of cologne. I hated the smell of men. Their scents caused my stomach to turn upside down. "Let me let you in on a little something, Jahrome. I got a CI that's placing you at each and every last one of these crime scenes. Through my CI, I've been able to connect all of the dots. Whether you talk to me or not, you're going down for each and every last one of these murders, unless you can tell me how to end this war between you and those goons from the wild hundreds. There are too many innocent lives being lost. You have the power to stop this shit. I suggest you do it, or you're going to spend an eternity in prison or hell real, real soon. You can bank on that."

I frowned and sucked my teeth at him. "I'm letting you know right now that I ain't dying in nobody's prison. I'm holding court right in them streets, officer. Where was all this passion when these bitch-niggas kilt my old man and popped my sister?" I adjusted myself in the hospital bed, not caring about the pain shooting through me. I was getting heated.

"Look, you blew me off. You said you didn't need my help, so I kept it moving. Some tough, punk-wannabe act like he got everything figured out, I'ma allow him to do things his way until he fails. In this case, you've failed big time. Not only is your stupid-ass in the hospital, but you've brought your mother and sister along for the ride. I don't understand how you're missing the big picture. The whole fucking city is after you. They want you dead. Two million dollars in cash is a lot of money. Do you realize how hard it is to make ends meet these days? Do you understand what a person can do with two million dollars in cash, here in Chicago?" he frowned.

The more he talked, the more heated I became. I was starting to get that me-against-the-world mentality. If muthafuckas wanted to come at me in the name of money, then it was up to me to survive by any and all means. I wasn't about to crumble. I didn't give a fuck what the stakes were.

"Look, I didn't need your help back then, and I don't need your shit now. I'm a muthafuckin' G until the death of me. So fuck you, and fuck yo' CI, and fuck all of the people in them pictures you showed. That's what it is. You wanna take me down yourself, righteous muthafucka, then get in line. I ain't telling you shit because I don't know shit," I snapped, feeling pain shoot all over my body. I felt like crying, it hurt so bad.

Taylor smiled and nodded his head. He backed away, walked to the door, and locked it. The next thing I knew, he was leaning over my bed before he grabbed me by the throat and pulled out his service weapon, placing it on my lips. "Open up! Now, you li'l bitch-ass nigger. Do it."

I closed my lips tighter and scrunched my face. I refused to open my mouth so he could put a gun down my throat. I didn't know who this fool thought he was dealing with, but I wasn't going. I'd rather he just started shooting.

He slammed his fist on my collarbone. *Bam*! It felt like the worst pain I could possibly imagine, like he'd broken it in two. My eyes got to watering, and then I was hollering at the top of my lungs before he slid his gun between my lips to muffle me. He slid it so far I gagged over the barrel.

"Now, you listen to me. I'm gon' give you a short pass so you can end this war that's happening in my city. There are too many women and children being killed. The streets are worse than ever, and it's all because of you. So, instead of me locking your ass up right now, I'ma let you roll yo' punk-ass out of here when they release you. If this war isn't ended within three months after you're out, I'm coming for your ass, boy. I make less than fifty thousand a year. Two million sounds real good right about now. You dig where I'm going with this?"

He pushed the gun further down my throat, holding his forearm under my Adam's apple. Anytime I tried to move in the slightest, the pain from my broken collarbone caused me to want to faint. I gagged around the barrel again and threw up some clear bile. I wanted to kill his bitch-ass. He was now added to my enemies list.

"Do you hear me? Huh? Say something!" he growled, forcing the gun down my throat so far I threw up all over my chest.

There was a pounding on the door. "Hey, it's been thirty minutes. Why is this door locked?" Yani yelled and proceeded to beat on it and call for the nurses.

Taylor forced his forearm into my neck even harder before stepping away from me with sweat pouring off his bald head. "I ain't always been no police. I was in these streets, too. I'm giving you three months after your release from this hospital. Fuck wit' me if you want to." He gathered his things, opened the door, and bumped Yani out of the way.

I wanted to jump out of my bed and run after him, but I was too busy coughing up a lung it felt like. My collarbone had been knocked back out of place. A couple of the bullet wounds had reopened and were bleeding. I felt so weak that all I could do was allow the tears to slide down my cheeks as I continued to choke.

Chapter 3

It was two more weeks before they released me from the hospital, and another three weeks before I was able to move around properly.

I knew I was too weak to go right at my foes, so Yani snatched up a small apartment two hours north of Chicago, across the border into a city called Milwaukee. It was located in the state of Wisconsin. I didn't know nothing about either the city or the state, and I didn't care to know about them. I was fully focused on my recovery and the recovery of my sister and mother.

Leah was up and running two weeks after we'd been ambushed. Her body had still been getting used to the pain medications they'd prescribed for her after being shot, which was the reason she'd passed out. Now her wound had healed up pretty nicely, and she was on low doses of the medication and seemed as good as new. I'd advised her to come out to Milwaukee with me and Yani until the beef died down in Chicago, even though I didn't know when that would be.

My mother, on the other hand, was not so good. When we were ambushed and the truck crashed into us, her leg had been caught, tangled up in the metal of my truck. The paramedics had to cut her out. Long story short, she'd lost her leg in the process. She, along with my sister and myself, was devastated.

If I thought she was heavy on the heroin before, she was going twice as hard now. It was enough to break my heart. No matter what I tried to say to her to make her feel better or see the positive side of things, nothing worked. The only thing that mattered to her was her dope.

***

I woke up one Thursday morning to Yani kissing all over my chest, circling my nipple with her tongue. I opened my eyes and glanced over at the digital clock on the night stand. It read 4:14 a.m. I rubbed the cold out of my eyes and looked up at her. "Baby, what's good?" My voice was raspy and dry as hell.

She continued to rub all over my chest. "I know you been down for a minute, but I'm horny. I need some of you before I drive back to the city for work. You think you can give me some?" She slid her hand between us and grabbed a handful of my dick, squeezing it in her small hand.

I closed my eyes and humped upward. My dick grew and began to pulsate. I gripped her big booty and rubbed all over it. She'd gotten thicker since I'd been down. The small, tight gown she wore was up around her ass cheeks. I could feel her hot pussy sitting on my left thigh. She humped into it, smearing her juices all over it.

She stroked me up and down. "What do you think, Daddy? You ready?"

I ran my hand all the way around and under her body, opening her thick sex lips with my fingers, sliding my middle finger deep into her oven, worming it in and out. "Hell yeah, boo. Get yo' thick ass up here and handle this bidness."

She whimpered. "Okay." She straddled me, leaned all the way over, and took ahold of my dick.

Kingpin Killaz 2

She ran the head in between her creases before slowly sitting down on it.

Her hot, slick walls sucked me in like a vacuum cleaner. I could feel how meaty she'd become down there.

"Uh. Heinous. I've missed this."

I held her waist while she rode me slowly at first, but gradually picked up speed, moaning loudly. I pulled down the straps of her gown to expose her big titties, cupped them, and sucked first the left brown nipple, then the right. They felt so soft and hot in my hands.

"Yes. Yes. Yes. Ooh. Yes, Daddy. Aw. My god!"

She placed her hands on my chest and rode me like a champion. Her back popped, ass jiggled, and breasts bounced on her frame.

The scent of her pussy drifted into the air and right up my nose. It smelled cleaned and natural. There was nothing like the natural scent of a woman's pussy to me, especially hers. It caused the animal to come out of me.

I gripped her waist and forced her to slam down on my piece, taking me as deep as she could. My eyes rolled to the back of my head. I found myself groaning from the feel of her insides. Those soft, pillow-y, tight muscles sucked and squeezed my pipe like a fist.

"Ride Daddy, Yani. Ride this dick, baby. Aw, fuck. You got that good pussy, boo. On my Blood, you do."

I dug my fingers into the meat of her fleshy ass and made her go into savage mode. I could hear her pussy slurping at my pipe. The noises were enough to drive me crazy.

"I'm about to cum! I'm about to cum! It's been so long! Shit. Aw, fuck! It's been so long. Here I cum!" she screamed.

She grabbed two handfuls of my chest and popped her pussy on my dick, juicing it, then she was shaking and cumming, trying to milk me already, but I was having none of that. I waited until she collapsed on me before I rolled her ass over and forced her thick thighs to her breasts. I guided myself back in and got to stabbing that wet pussy while her juices leaked out of her and slid down her ass crack. Her thick thighs felt hot on my shoulders. I lowered myself until we were cheek-to-cheek, then my dick was plunging in and out of her hot pocket, thrusting and long-stroking that gushy pussy. Stuffing her.

"Aw. My God. Jesus. Please. Daddy. You. Fucking me. So. Hard. Shit!" she whimpered.

I rolled my back, sliding as deep as I could, and pulled out only to slam back home. My sack crashing against her ass over and over. I sucked all over her sweaty neck, and my long tongue played on her earlobe as I played around inside of her. That pussy was so good I didn't want to stop. Yani had that good-good ever since we were in high school.

"Daddy, I'm cumming again! I'm cumming again. Aw, fuck! It's so good!"

I timed her shakes. I felt her walls close around my penis, and then I was coming deep within her womb. "Uh! Uh! Yani! Fuck, boo. Fuck. Daddy cumming. I'm cumming!" I hollered, jerking with each spurt of my semen into her hot womb. It was amazing. There wasn't nothing like that good hood fucking where both parties fucked like they had something to prove.

I fell on top of her and slowly rolled to my side, my dick sticking straight up in the air. She grabbed it and sucked the head into her mouth, sucking her juices from it loudly. The noises immediately got to me. Instead of my penis deflating, it got harder and harder until I came down her throat. She swallowed it and continued to suck, pumping me with her small fist.

I had to pull her ass up my body and wrap my arms around her. We breathed heavily into each other's faces. I rubbed all over her juicy booty, smacking the cheeks just to see them jiggle by the sunlight peaking in through the window.

"What are you going to do with that million in cash you had me grab from the hotel?" She kissed me and nuzzled her face into the crux of my neck.

"That money gon' be used to make sure you women are good while I'm down in Chicago handling my bidness. I don't give a fuck what I'm doing, y'all gotta stay straight at all times. That's my job. You feel me?" I slid my hand all the way between her legs so I could feel her heat again. I pinched her clit and pulled on it. I loved doing that.

"Mm, stop, Heinous, I'm trying to say something to you if you'll let me finish. You know I can't handle you touchin' on me like that. I've never been able to."

I slid my middle finger into her back door and held it there. "A'ight, boo, g'on 'head. Tell me what's on your mind."

She squeezed her eyes together and slid her hand

between her legs, squishing the lips of her pussy together. "Ok, damn, what was I finna say? Oh, yeah. Why won't you just use that million dollars to hit it from Chicago? I mean, it ain't nothing but heartache and pain in that city. That and death. There is no place for us there any longer. This money may be God's way of trying to save us. Can't we look at it that way and be smart? I don't want to lose you. You're all I have."

I popped my middle finger out of her ass and sighed, shaking my head. "Baby, I wish it was that simple. But them pigs kilt my pops, shot my sister, and got my mother's leg cut off. Not to mention how many slugs I done ate so far. I can't take that shit lying down. I'd never be able to live with myself if I even tried to. I gotta finish what I started, besides, Brat needs me. She just lost her whole family, and I have been there to support her. You know they was killed on my behalf, right?"

She nodded. "Yeah, I get all of that. But I need you. Your mother needs you, as well as Leah. I mean, not that Brat doesn't, but her people are already gone. There is no use fighting for the dead when you still have to protect the living. I'm driving myself crazy thinking about you every second of every day, even when you're right in my face. I think it'd be stupid for you to go back down there on some kamikaze-type shit. You should be way smarter than that. Seriously, bae." She slid from my embrace and got out of the bed, sliding her gown over her head. She looked over her shoulder at me. "Don't you love me, Heinous?"

I blew air out of my jaws and sat up. I needed to

think. Not only was I starting to feel pain, but the heroin was calling me like never before. Yani was stressing me out. I didn't feel like thinking about all of that shit right then.

"Yani, you know I love you, boo. I been loving you ever since we were kids. That ain't never gon' change. You're my world." I got out of the bed and pulled her into my embrace. My penis slapped against my thighs before she smashed it with her own.

"If I'm your world, you would listen to me. We need to move forward, not backward. By the grace of God we were able to walk out of that city on our own volition. Well, there's your mother, of course, but at least she still has her life. And life is so fucking short, Jahrome! Damn! Why can't you see that? A million dollars can do so much for us. Let's start over. I am begging you with my whole heart," she pleaded.

There were two knocks on the door, then Leah pushed it in and stepped into the room. "What is all the racket going on in here? Damn, we still trying to sleep out there." She looked from me to Yani with a frown on her pretty face.

Yani wiggled away from me once again and stood beside my sister, leaving me naked and exposed. "This fool planning on going back to Chicago to war with Pesos and the rest of the city. You need to try and talk some sense into him, because I can't get through to him, even though he swearing up and town he love me and shit." She rolled her eyes and crossed her arms in front of her chest, tapping her pedicured toes on the carpet.

Leah stepped forward and hugged me. "Bro, tell

35

me she lying. That ain't true, is it?" She lay her head on my chest.

"Leah, come on, man. You already know how I get down. I can't let them niggas get off on me like that. They popped you, cut mom's leg off, kilt our old man, and hit me up. Nall, I ain't going. They gon' have to kill me before I bow down to their gangsta. That's on everything I love, including our blood." I kissed her forehead, stepped away, and pulled my boxers on.

She stepped back in front of me and blinked back tears. "Are you fucking kidding me? You're going to go back into some death trap to prove a point to yourself? Really?" She squinted at me as if she couldn't believe what she was hearing.

"Y'all ain't gotta worry about nothing. I'ma make sure y'all good while I'm handling my bidness. Once I knock that fool Pesos' head from his shoulders, it's gon' be what I'm doing. If I don't squash these cock suckers, we gon' have to worry about them for the rest of our lives. I can't have that. I don't like looking over my shoulders."

She blew air through her teeth and grabbed my chin aggressively. "You, you, you. That's all I'm hearing right now. What about us, Jahrome? Huh? You ever stop to think about us?"

Now I was getting irritated. I couldn't believe she'd ask me some shit like that. Everything I did was for them. I never thought about me until after the women in my circle were taken care of. I'd been that way ever since I was a real li'l dude.

"Look, Leah. You talking real stupid right now. Everything I do is for the safety and security of this family. I been making sure you was straight since before I could remember. You coming at me real sideways right now. Straight-up." I slid my wife beater over my head, then put on my ankle socks. I didn't know what I was getting dressed for. It wasn't like I was about to go somewhere in the city we were in. I didn't know my way around it, or what types of goons were lurking. I was a Chicago nigga, born and bred, so I thought every city in America was like the one I was from.

After getting dressed, I tried to slide past Leah, but she held my arm. I yanked it away from her and a sharp pain shot up through my collarbone, nearly hobbling me. I fell to one knee, grabbing it.

"Jahrome, are you okay?" Leah asked, dropping to her knees beside me. She placed her hand on my shoulder with her eyes wide open.

I shook my head real slowly. "I'm good. I gotta get the fuck out of here, though. Y'all are driving me crazy." I opened my mini-safe, taking out fifty thousand dollars. I gave twenty-five thousand to Leah and the other twenty-five to Yani.

"Look, I know y'all mean well and all of that shit, but I gotta do what I gotta do. I can't be alive if them niggas are, too. I won't be able to rest peacefully until that nigga Pesos and Lost Boy are six feet under. That's just the way it is. I'll see y'all in a couple days." I kissed Leah on the cheek, and Yani on the lips. She was crying her little heart out, and so was my sister, but I'd made my mind up. I had to do what I had to.

I stepped out of the room and into my mother's bedroom. Hers was dark with the exception of a small candle burning on her dresser. She sat in a rocking chair beside the dresser, humming along to a Luther Vandross song. "I guess you tired of arguing with those girls, huh?" She laughed to herself, and wiped her nose with the palm of her hand.

The candle flickered bright enough for me to see the works that were on top of the dresser. Her room smelled of funk, as much as I hated to admit it. This was heart-wrenching to me because my mother had always been a very clean and pleasantly-scented woman. Her appearance was one of her top priorities. In fact, while growing up I heard about it so much that it was drilled into my head. I remember she'd stressed the importance of that to me, especially whenever I got dirt on my clothes when I was really, really little. Leah would do the same.

"Ma, I gotta go back to the city so I can handle some business. I'll be back in a few days, okay?" I knelt on the side of her and picked up her right hand, kissing the back of it.

She nodded. "Well, sugar, you gotta do what you gotta do. It ain't for a woman to stand in a man's way of his destiny. If you feel like you have unfinished business, son, then you gotta do what you gotta do. Me, personally, I don't think you should go down there, either. I feel like the reaper is waiting for your return. You know that whole city is against you. But the battle starts in the spiritual realm. I don't like the odds, baby. But, once again, I can't tell you what to do. You must use your third eye more than the two on your face. You understand me?"

I nodded and kissed her hand again. "I gave Leah and Yani each a nice amount. If you need anything, hit my phone, Ma. I mean that. You're my Queen."

She smiled and laid her hand on the top of my head, rubbing my waves. "I know I am, baby. I'll tell you what I need. When you come back, make sure you have Mama some of her medicine. The best you can find. The quality of work in Wisconsin is trash, not even fifty percent. I'm fie'ning."

I kissed her hand and stood up. "I got you. Just take it easy with that stuff you got. I know I can't tell you what to do, so I won't even try. We understand each other. That's what I've always loved about our relationship."

I kissed her forehead, then hugged her as tight as I could. Being so close, I could really smell her funk. I felt like my heart was being ripped in two.

Hood Rich

Kingpin Killaz 2

Chapter 4

Brat took the Mach .11 out of the green crate and pulled the clip out of it, looking it over. "Nigga, they been on my ass ever since you went down. They shot up my mother, brother, and nieces, and kilt two of Bam-Bam's li'l homies from the projects. The city been going crazy, nigga. That's why I had to call in a few favors, nigga, from my cousins out of Cali. It's a whole crate of these pretty bitches. Watch," she exclaimed, tapping the trigger and activating a red beam located on the top of the Mach. "This bitch been rigged to shoot rapidly. All these clips hold a hundred rounds."

I rubbed the alcohol pad on my inner forearm until I located a nice, thick vein, then stuck the needle directly into it before injecting the heroin into my system. What I was shooting was eighty percent pure. The flow was smooth and potent. It caused my eyes to roll backward and my lids to flutter over them. It felt like I was experiencing a hundred orgasms at one time.

Brat came over and set up her work before shooting some of the drug. She'd started after her family was killed in cold blood, the pain of their loss becoming too much for her to endure. I watched her eyes roll back, then she scooted back in her chair with her mouth open and her eyes closed.

"I feel like you left me stranded, Heinous. I had to deal with all of this shit on my own, nigga. That ain't how we get down. You know that." She wiped her nose and smacked her lips.

I opened mine slowly, feeling the drug take me

higher and higher. We were seated in her living room. There was big screen television playing in the corner, but neither one of us was paying any attention to it. "Brat, I could never leave you, dawg, and you know that. Them niggas not only fucked me over, but they hit my people, too. I was in the hospital, then after that I needed to recuperate. You know how this shit go. We been warring and killing since the beginning. Just me and you, my nigga." I grabbed the Mach off table and looked it over. I could feel the power of it. I imagined me busting it until the clip was empty. I couldn't wait to kill again. I needed to make my enemies feel my pain on so many levels

Brat ran her tongue across her dry lips. She had her head shaved into a curly mohawk. Her face was without makeup, though her eyebrows were done. She frowned. "We gon' off these niggas' heads, Heinous. I'm ready to start killing up some shit right now. I got the low-down on where that fool Pesos laying his head. I'm fucking the same bitch as him right now. I say we mount and go at his chin tonight. He gon' be at my bitch crib. She stay out in Riverdale. Say he gon' slide through later on tonight in the wee hours. What you think?"

I was so high that I could hear my heart pounding in my chest. There was a soft jazz song playing in my head that I had never heard before, but each chord was performed so perfectly. I could feel the blood as it flowed from my heart and into my veins. "I don't trust no nigga. I don't trust no bitch," I slurred and dosed off. I awoke thirty seconds later. "How long have you known this bitch? How do you know she ain't in it for the two million dollars?"

Brat wiped her nose again and sniffed. She grabbed the bottle of Hennessy off of the table and turned it up, guzzling it. She slammed the bottle on top of the table and burped. "Heinous, I been wetting shit as long as you have. You talking to me like I'm one of these rookie killas. You know I ain't no bitch. That shit make a mockery of us." She turned the bottle back up and stood. "I been getting this ho for a year now. I know what she's capable of. I know all of her strengths and weaknesses. Anytime she's been down and all, I've been the one stepping up to the plate to make sure her and her son were straight. That nigga Pesos would let her starve, and has on multiple occasions. This bitch only fucking wit' him out of fear, not passion or love. Trust me."

I took the Mach, tapped the trigger, and activating the red beam, shining it on the wall. "Nigga, you the only one I trust. I just hope you know there is a lot at stake here."

Brat laughed and drank another long swallow of alcohol. She staggered back and forth on her feet Her eyes were low. "They got two million on your head, and one on mine. I know what's at stake here. You can believe that. Now, I'm ready to off this fuck-nigga, Heinous. Tell me you're with me? That's all I need to know."

I placed the Mach on the table and sat back in the seat, spreading my legs. "I'm down with you, Brat, but if we gon' kill this nigga, we gon' fuck him over royally. I'm talking make a spectacle of his ass. I want niggas to talk about his murder all over town for years and years to come. Then I wanna finish Lost Boy and School Boy. Both of them niggas gotta go.

That's just the way it is. Both of them niggas done crossed us."

"They killed my mother, Heinous. They killed my muthafucking mother. Damn, she was all I had." She fell to her knees in tears.

As long as I had known her, I'd never seen her break down as such. It hit me directly in the heart. I had to ride for her and myself. I owed us that.

I got out of the chair and knelt beside her, putting my arm around her shoulder. "You know I got you. We can do shit however you want to. Long as you feel deep within your soul that you can trust this bitch, then I'ma follow yo' lead. But if I see anything out of the ordinary, I'ma do what I gotta do. I'm letting you know that right now." I hugged her tighter.

She bowed her head and cried into the palms of her hands. Tears slid down her wrists and dropped to the carpet. She shook her head from side to side. "My mother, Heinous. My mother, man? Who else I got? They killed my mother and my brother. Who else I got in this world? Don't nobody give a fuck about Brat." She threw my arms off of her and sat back at the table. She took the drugs and got her works together before drawing it up into her syringe. She tied a belt around her right arm and smacked it, finding the vein that formed there. She grabbed the syringe and stuck the needle into it, pushing down on the feeder.

Her eyes rolled backward. She closed her eyelids tight and groaned. Releasing the belt, she dropped it to the carpet. Drool slid out of the corner of her mouth.

I took the bottle of Hennessy and sipped out of it I really didn't like the taste, but my throat was drier than the desert. I was super high already. I needed to take a seat. The music in my head was playing so loud I couldn't think straight.

I placed my arm on the table and laid my face in it. I just needed to take a quick nap, maybe for ten minutes, then I would be good. I was sure of it.

"You don't give a fuck about me, Heinous. Nigga, you left me," Brat said in a raspy voice.

I didn't even look up at her. I didn't feel like hearing that emotional shit. She was high and going through some thangs. I wasn't gon' feed into it. I took my .40 Glock out of my waistband and sat it in my lap because with the way I was hunched over, the handle of the gun was poking me in my lower abdomen, and that was killing me. After I situated it, I was good to go.

"Brat, take a nap. You're tripping right now." I got into a comfortable position with my face in my arms and got ready to take a short nap when I heard the sound of a gun cocking.

"Nigga, I said you don't give no fucks about me. And since you don't, then I don't give no fucks about you."

I picked my head up out of my arms and looked across the table at her. She had the Mach .11 aimed at me with a mug on her face and tears coming out of her eyes. "What's your last words, Heinous? What you want me to tell your sister?" she asked with tears coming out of her eyes and snot out of her nose.

I eyed the Mach, and then looked up at her. "This what we on now? You aiming guns at me and shit, huh?" I felt my blood pressure rising. My high was lowering, yet the music wouldn't stop playing in my head.

"Nigga, you left me in that parking lot to be killed. Then, after that, you went on the run to Milwaukee. You wasn't thinking about me. You were only thinking about yourself and your family. Admit that shit, nigga? Admit it, and let's get this whole thing over with." She tapped the trigger of the Mach. The beam cast a red dot on my forehead. I trailed my eyes upward, locating it before looking back over at her.

"So what, you gon' kill me now? You hurting so much in your heart from what these bitch-niggas did to us that it's gon' make you kill me, the last real piece of family you got, Blood? Really?" Now I was getting vexed. I was starting to see her in a completely different light. We both lived by the rules to never pull a gun out on a nigga unless we were going to use it to body them. Knowing Brat, I knew she had every intention of using her weapon. That is what hurt me the most. I was feeling like I was going to have to kill my best friend and right-hand.

Brat curled her upper lip. "You ain't my brother no mo', Heinous. Nigga, you left me for dead. Wouldn't no brother of mine do that to me. Besides, all of this shit that's going on is your fault. Had you never allowed your pops to go out to the Gardens after knowing how they got down out there, we would've never been beefing with Pesos. And had you never popped off at the mouth, we wouldn't have half of the Bloods on our asses. This red shit is all we know. Now we can't even turn to the fucking family that raised us. It's been one bad decision after the next with you. Decisions that got my mother, brother and nieces slain. So nall, nigga, you ain't no brother of mine no more."

She scooted her chair back and swiped the bottle of Hennessy from the table, taking long swallows from it. I scrunched my face and eyed her with mounting anger. "If that's how you feel, bust then. You sitting here whining of this bullshit like you done gave up. Talking like I'm the enemy when I been riding beside yo' punk-ass ever since we were li'l-ass kids. I've always had your back. Always for you. You think I would have left you out on purpose or if I wasn't fucked up? Huh?" I slid my hand around the grip of my gun and cocked the hammer. Somebody wasn't leaving this room, and I wasn't about to let it be me. I loved Brat with all my heart, but I loved me and my family more.

Brat eyed my gun. She shook her head. "You got them killed, Heinous. All of them. Now it's on my conscious. You got me doing dope and shit. Nall. I should have never followed you. It was stupid of me to do so all of these years."

She took another swallow from the bottle, jumped up, and went to set the Mach on the table, but it was too late. As soon as I saw her jump up, I thought she was on bullshit, so I scooted my chair all the way back and fell backward onto the floor, finger-fucking my Glock and sending three slugs into her chest and two to her stomach. She flew back into the wall and slid down it with her eyes wide open in shock. The bottle of liquor crashed to the floor and spilled its contents beside her.

I jumped up with my gun smoking, the scent of gunpowder heavy in the air. I threw the table out of the way and looked down on her with my gun aimed at her forehead. "Why the fuck you do this, Brat? Damn, man. You my nigga," I cried.

She kicked her right leg and ran her hand over the holes in her chest and abdomen. Blood coated her fingers and leaked out of the corners of her mouth. Her eyes blinked rapidly. "You shot me, Heinous. You shot me," she rasped, so softly I could barely hear her. Her right leg continue to kick as a pool of blood formed around her.

I fell to my knees in it, feeling horrible. I felt sick. I dry-heaved and almost threw up on her lap. I couldn't believe what I had done. My Queens had been right. I should've never came back to Chicago. it was a stupid decision that had cost Brat her life.

"Brat. Aw, fuck. I'm sorry, man. I'm sorry." I laid her down flat and ripped her beater down the middle. I could see the three big holes in her chest. Blood spurted out of them like running faucets. Below them, the two holes in stomach did the same. She was losing so much blood that I new there was no chance of her making it.

She held her mouth wide open, trying to talk to me. She lifted her hand in the air toward me. It shook with blood dripping off of it. "Hei. Heinou. I'm sor." She started to shake and cough up globs of blood, then she clutched her chest and tried to scream, but all that came out was more blood.

I grabbed her neck and placed the barrel of the Glock against her forehead, pulling the trigger. One shot. One shell hopped out of the gun and landed on the carpet, smoking.

I scooted away from her, placed my gun on the floor and rocked back and forth while I looked over her dead body. I couldn't believe I had killed her. My best friend. The only person in this world who I knew would enter into the tall shadow of death beside me. Brat. My ace. She was dead, and it was all because of me.

I broke down crying for ten minutes straight. Her puddle of blood had made its way to me and saturated the seat of my Ferragamo jeans. It took forever for me to feel that before I snapped out of it.

I stood up and tucked my pistol back on my waist. I walked to her body. I could already smell the death of it. Her eyes were open and crossed, the top of her head blown off, its fragments all over the wall and carpet around her. I stepped over her body and grabbed my works. I couldn't leave my blood at this scene. I also grabbed the bottle of Hennessy since I'd drank out of it, and then I wiped down everything I thought I touched, and even stuff I knew I didn't.

I rushed downstairs to Brat's bedroom and flipped her mattress and box spring over, then pushed her side table out of the way. I knelt down, and hit the wall to the right of her dresser, about six inches from the floor. It popped out. I moved the wall panel aside, and five minutes later was able to get her safe out of it. It was about three feet long and two feet wide. I knew the code was her mother's birthday, so two minutes later I had it open and was filling the pillowcase off of her bed with money and dope. I mean, it wasn't like she needed it anymore.

By the time I got back into the living room, there

were two big-ass rats gnawing away at her face. I stomped my foot at them and they hissed at me with foam coming out of their mouths. That was all I had to see, and I was like 'fuck that.'

When I got back to my truck, I jumped in and tossed the money and dope into my back seat before breaking down, crying and shouting at the top of my lungs. I couldn't believe I had offed my best friend. What the fuck had I been thinking? She was dead because of me. I knew I would never be the same again.

Chapter 5

I closed the door to my mother's room and locked it. I was fresh from a shower, and only five hours prior I'd killed Brat. I needed to leave this world, if only through my drug usage. I flipped on her light. She had been sitting in the rocking chair, nodding off. When the light came on, she perked up and held her hand up to block its brightness. "What are you doing, boy?"

I sat on her bed and placed the quarter kilo onto her nightstand. "I got that good work, this is more than eight five percent. It had to be more than a half ounce. You gon' love this." I took a portion and started to get the work ready.

My mother looked over at me and frowned. "Wait, baby, what are you doing? I know you ain't messing with this stuff, are you?"

"I need it, Mama. I just did something tonight that's going to haunt me for the rest of my life. I can't take what's going on with me right now. I'm about to lose my freaking mind. Seriously." I poked the needle into my vein and fed the dope into my system. As soon as it entered me, I started to shake with euphoria. My eyes watered. I closed them and smiled.

I sat with my back against the headboard, took the remote from her bed, and activated the stereo. Luther Vandross' *If This World Were Mine* began to bellow out of the speaker. I found the song calming and soothing. It was just what I needed.

"Uh!" My mother groaned, shooting the heroin into her own arm. She laid her head back on the rocking chair and set the syringe on the night table beside the remainder of her dope. "Baby, that feel so good."

Ten seconds later I could hear her snoring loudly. My chin fell to my chest. Drool came out of the corners of my mouth. Even though I was sleeping, I was awake and fully alert. I was actually singing along to the Luther song, even though my eyes were closed and I was snoring. For some reason heroin always had me like that. I could be nodded out, yet at the same time fully aware of everything that was going on in the room.

"You wanna talk about it, sugar?" my mother asked.

I opened my eyes and looked over at her. She was lighting five candles and setting them in strategic places all around the room on her side. Well, places she could reach while sitting in her rocking chair. After they were all placed, she got up and turned off the light, hopping on one leg, then she sat back in her chair, scratching her neck like crazy.

Because I saw her itching her neck, it made my skin begin to itch. Then my injection site was itching like crazy, so I tore at it. It felt like bugs were trying to crawl under my skin.

"I did something tonight, and it's killing me." I sniffed snot back into my nose and shook my head. "I don't know if it was the right thing to do or not, Mama. I messed up."

The Luther track changed over to *Wait for Love.*

She smiled. "Baby, we all make mistakes. I knew before you went back down to Chicago that something very serious was going to take place. I been seeing tombstones in all my dreams. That means death. Somebody very close to us is going to be fatally hurt. I just don't know who, but I think you do. In fact, I know you do. The Angel of Death is all over you, even right now."

She wiped her nose again and winced in pain as she picked up her lonely leg and placed it on the night table. "Tell me what is going on, son. Confession is good for the soul. If it's one thing that Mama knows, it's that."

The image of Brat's blown head popped into my mind. The multiple gunshot wounds in her torso. Fatal wounds I had caused. I felt myself getting sick again. I hopped out of the bed and fell to my knees, dry heaving over my mother's waste basket. Every time I heaved, my stomach felt as if it was in knots. No food came up, only a line of spit. It had been two days since I'd eaten anything. Heroin kept me feeling full even though there was no logical way I could be.

I wiped my mouth with the back of my hand and sat on my haunches. "I killed Brat, Mama. Today. I shot her six times and took her life. I thought she was about to kill me, and it happened." Tears ran down my cheeks now. I couldn't stop them from coming.

My mother held her arms out to me. "Come here, baby. Let Mama hold you."

I crawled across the floor and sat my head in her lap. My mother smelled horrible. I could tell she'd not taken care of her hygiene in any way ever since she'd gotten out of the hospital. Her scent was so bad I was struggling to breathe. But as bad as it was, I remained with my head in her lap because I needed her affection. I needed my mother.

Hood Rich

She rubbed my face and kissed me on the side of my forehead. "I want you to ask our Father in Heaven for forgiveness and move on with your life, baby. I know that is easier said than done, but you cannot allow one death to be responsible for two. Meaning you've killed her, now you're lettin' the death of her, or your guilt because of it, kill you. Get over it, baby."

I was in full-on tears. I kept seeing me and Brat in the ninth grade, fighting side-by-side with one another. Then, years later, us busting our guns together and flipping bad bitches in the same bed. Hustling together and struggling together. She was my rider. I knew that for a fact. Now I'd misjudged her intentions and took her life. I was fucked up.

"You don't understand, Ma. You see, I thought she was about to shoot me down, when in actuality she was setting her gun back on the table. I misjudged her."

She kissed my forehead again and nodded off for two minutes. I mean snoring loudly, too. Then, all once, she snapped out of it. "Now, you listen to me, son. We can't afford you having my addiction or my paranoia. Either way, she's gone. I'm sick of this shit. Excuse my language. You're laying on me crying because of what happened to her, but look at where your head is. I'm suppose to have a whole-ass leg right there, but I don't. It's missing. Why? because shit happens to people every damn day. You just have to grit your teeth and bare it. Life goes on. Period. Now, I need you to get your butt up and turn into a man. I've already got a daughter. Brat is dead. So is her mother. So is her brother and them little girls. Move on." She pushed my head off of her lap and grabbed her works. "I don't want to hear about this shit no more. I'm not playing, either. Take it to God, ask for forgiveness, then move on. I swear if I hear about it again, I'm gon' take my only leg and put it so far up your ass that you'll be brushing your teeth and my toes every morning. Now g'on, get. You're stressing me out." she waved me away.

My mother made me feel like a straight wimp. I wanted to question if I was supposed to feel as much remorse as I felt for Brat or if I was overdoing it on some soft shit like she was making it seem. I mean, it was still the same day. Didn't I have a right to feel how I felt about a friend I'd known ever since I was a kid? I shook my head and grabbed the work, leaving her a little more of it, before bouncing.

I exited the bedroom door and bumped into Leah. She had tears in her eyes.

"Dang, Brat dead? Why did you have to do that to her? Y'all were cool, Jahrome." She grabbed two handfuls of my shirt and fell against me.

I picked her up. She wrapped her legs around my hips and placed her face in the crux of my neck while I rubbed her back, bouncing her up and down as if she was still a little girl. Tears fell from my eyes again. "I thought she was about to kill me, sis. She pulled a Mach on me. Put the beam on my forehead and everything. Said I wasn't her brother no more. I saw death in her eyes. She said it was my fault her people go murdered. That she was tired of following me. Then she hopped up with the Mach in her hand. Before she could pop me, I had to handle my bidness. Don't be mad at me, Leah. I need you right now."

I continued to hold her. Her sobbing got louder. Her and Brat had been real close, even to the point they had slept together more than a few times over the years. I knew her death would hit my sister hard, and it did.

"I just don't understand. Y'all was so cool. Y'all been through everything together. Everything. She was like our sister. Now she's gone. Just dead like everybody else. Why?"

I carried her into my bedroom and laid her on the bed, her head against the headboard. Then I climbed on the side of her and wrapped my arms around her waist, pulling her back to me and spooning as if we were kids again. "I'm sorry, Leah. You know I loved her, too. I would have never done that if she didn't make it seem like she was about to come at me. You know my heart. Right, sis?"

She continued to cry for another five minutes, then gradually it tapered off. She turned all the way around until she was facing me and placed her forehead against mine. Tears continued to fall. She put her right hand on my shoulder. "I'm just glad it wasn't you, Jahrome. Like, what if she did lure you back to Chicago so she could kill you? What would I do then, huh? We've already lost Mama. That dope has her, so we're all we really have." She rubbed my cheek and then kissed my lips before placing her forehead against them.

"Hey, what about me? Y'all still have me. I ain't goin' nowhere," Yani said, standing in the open doorway with a bowl of cereal in her hands. She set it on the dresser and climbed into the bed until she was lying behind Leah. Once there, she kissed her on the back of the neck. "You okay, little sister?"

Leah closed her eyes and moaned. "Yeah, me and Jahrome was just talking about some stuff. Nothing too major. I'm good."

Leah rolled and laid on her back, and Yani climbed on top of her, straddling her body before kissing all over her lips. Yani had on these real small, red, lace boy shorts that were all up in her ass. With her bent over the way she was, I could see the majority of her pussy and all of her cheeks, and her monkey print from the back. I snuck my head in between her legs and sniffed her box, then licked the material, tasting her juices through it just enough to drive me crazy.

She arched her back and moaned. "Uh, what you back there doing?"

I pulled the material to the side and licked in between her creases. I slurped her juices and opened her ass cheeks and pussy lips at the same time, sucking on both holes. Leah placed her hands on Yani's ass and pulled the cheeks apart for me to do my thing. I could see her fingers playing in Yani's slit. The middle went inside of her and slid back and forth.

Yani moaned. "Un-uh, y'all not about to do this to mc."

Leah held her pussy lips open, and I licked all around her fingers, found Yani's clit, and sucked on it before flickering it with my tongue from side-to-side. Her essence poured out of her and dropped onto Leah's panties. Yani humped into Leah's covered mound. Both girls began to moan loudly. That drove me crazy.

I slid my tongue as far into Yani as it could go. Yani pulled Leah's shirt over her head, then rose and allowed Leah's tongue to meet Yani's. Their lips squished together, ground hard at one another.

Leah moaned. "Aw, fuck, Yani. Damn, that shit feel good." She held her head with both hands. Yani was pulling her thick nipples with her teeth, then sucking them into her mouth. She went from one breast to the next.

My tongue went in and out of Yani's fat lips. Her juices coated my chin and upper lip. I could taste her on my tongue, and it excited me. There was nothing like the taste of pussy. I pulled my pipe out and ran it up and down her slit before ramming into her.

She jerked her head back. "Uh! Fuck! I thought you was gon' let us play. Shit! Fuck me! Fuck me hard, Daddy!" She slammed back into me and continued to kiss all over Leah, squeezing her titties and sucking on the hard nipples.

I smacked her ass cheeks hard, ripped most of her lace boy shorts off of her, and kept on fucking and going as deep as I possibly could while Leah rubbed all over her ass and held her pussy lips apart for me. That made me go into savage mode. This wasn't the first time me and Leah had flipped Yani. Since Yani and I had been together, it had happened a lot. Even though she made it seem like she didn't like it, she loved it.

I was sure she was about to cum hard in a matter of seconds, so I sped up the pace and got to waxing that ass.

"Aw. Aw. Daddy. You so deep. You so deep. I'm cumming. I'm cumming!" She slammed back into me as hard as she could, and I met her thrust-for-thrust, gripped her fleshy ass cheeks for leverage. She was so thick that all of her was jiggling and shaking. That was doing something to me.

When she started to cum, she locked up and fell on top of Leah, but continued to hump back into me, twerking in my lap.

Leah got on top of her and sucked all over Yani's breasts and fingered her pussy fast and hard. Then she opened her thighs wide, turned a bit sideways, and got to rubbing her pussy against hers while she held her lips apart. Her ass flexed as she did her thing. "Un. Un. Un. Yani. You got a fat ass. Damn, you do. And you stay wet, like me."

I stroked my pipe and fed it to Yani. She turned her head to the side and sucked it into her mouth, deep throating it like a champion while she moaned within her throat.

Leah continued to work her hips. She threw her head back and let out a guttural cry before cumming all over Yani. She lay on her back, fingering herself while Yani abandoned my pipe to suck her breasts and lick all over her stomach and neck.

They sixty-nined, slurping all over each other loudly. My dick throbbed with anger. The stuffy room was heavily scented with sweat and pussy. I was yearning for more.

Once Leah began to eat Yani, I played in her juices and coated my dick with them just before I slowly eased into Yani's asshole, inch-by-inch. I worked myself in and out of her while she moaned and whimpered. Leah continued to eat Yani's pussy, sucking on her clit and bringing her to another orgasm.

When it was all said and done, both Leah and Yani came so much back-to-back that the room reeked of natural scents.

Yani lay back with her cheek against mine, and before she passed out, she slid her tongue into my mouth, sucking all over my lips. "I love you. I'm so glad you're home and safe. You're my everything." She yawned and fell out.

***

Early the next morning, I was awakened by Yani shaking my chest.

"Bae! Wake up. That nigga School Boy outside. I don't know how he found us, but he did. He outside right now in a black Hummer," She hollered with eyes wide open.

Leah had her leg wrapped around me. I pushed it off, got up, and threw my clothes on quick. I snapping my bullet proof vest into place and threw two .40 Glocks on my hips. I was feeling sicker than ever. The heroin was calling me. I needed my morning fix. I felt like I had to shit and throw up at the same time. There were also stabbing pains in my abdomen.

But none of that stopped me from making it to the door with a mug on my face. I stepped out into the 5:00 a.m. morning. There were birds chirping and singing in the tree in front of the duplex. It must've rained the night before, because the ground and the atmosphere were very misty-like. I could also smell rain and morning dew. My Jordans had very little traction on the wet porch.

I jogged down the stairs and approached the Hummer, ready to air that bitch out if I had to. I knew School Boy was a snake by nature. One of the reasons he was tracking me down was because he wanted me to off his right-hand mans and smoke his baby mother. This nigga was a fool.

Before I could make it all the way to the tinted Hummer. The driver's door opened and School Boy's tall-ass stepped out of it with a pair of Torn Ford sunglasses and an all-black Gucci fit with the red bandana around his neck. He wore red and black Airmax 95s. His neck was also full of gold and diamonds.

He threw his arms in the air. "What's good, Jo? I know you ain't tryna run from a nigga?"

Hood Rich

Chapter 6

"Now that you out of the hospital, it's time we started. The city is already on its heels. They don't know what to expect or who gon' get hit next. They the ones who put the bounty on yo' head up to two and a half million. I think the cartel got something to do with that, though. The last I heard, all the warring in Chicago was preventing them from making an ample amount of money. It's all about business for them. They feeling like if they can make more money with you dead and gone, then that's the route they'll take. I don't give a fuck about them. I'm concerned about this nigga Lost Boy. He tryin' to get up with them Kings out of Crown Town. A lot of them just getting over here from Mexico. If he do that, he'll be more powerful than ever because he'll have Mexican connects. We can't allow that, or should I say 'I can't allow that.' I want this nigga's head taken off ASAP. You gotta handle that bidness, and you gotta let it be known it was you. Muthafuckas will really tremble. I'ma put you up on game about this fuck boy, where he gon' be at tomorrow night wit' my B.M. You can handle two birds with one stone right then. You feel me?" School Boy tooted a line of cocaine and coughed. He pinched his nostrils.

He hadn't mentioned how he found me or his stay in Milwaukee. The only thing running through my head was upping my pistol and putting two in his face.

"Blood, how the fuck you find me? And don't give no bullshit-ass response. I want the truth," I snapped, slidin' my hand under my shirt. I didn't

Hood Rich

know how good the security was in the hotel, but I was about to take my chances. This nigga was better off dead.

"Aw, it wasn't hard. I knew you couldn't get by wit'out money. I'd be good as dead if you asked me. I had to break away from them, especially now that Brat was gone. If this fuck-nigga just find me like he had, then that meant he's off me. Yo' bitch goin' back and forth to your shops to keep them running smoothly, as well as her own. All I had to do was follow her out of the city. She led me right to your duck-off. Nigga, I also followed you back here the other night after you smoked Brat in her crib. It's amazing how comfortable you are. I didn't do no fancy driving or none of that. You just overlooked me riding behind you. Why you smoke yo' homie, anyway? She been getting on your nerves or some shit?" He laughed and pulled his big nose, sniffing loudly as most tooters do.

A chill went down my spine. My heart skipped a beat, then started to beat faster and faster. I took a seat on the bed across from him. "I don't know what you talking about. I ain't kill nobody the other night. You bugging."

He laughed and waved me off. "Aw, nigga, fuck that bitch. What you don't know is she took a million dollars to set you up. Had you been there fifteen minutes longer, Pesos and his would have been there to lay you down. That niggas was on the way to light you up like Times Square. Bitch ain't have yo' back, Blood. And she murdered her own people." He laughed again and took a Newport out of his pocket, lighting it. He blew the smoke toward the ceiling.

As soon as the smoke reached my nose, I cringed. I hated the smell of cigarettes. "Fuck you mean, she kilt her own people? What type of sense that make? She loved her mother with all of her heart, Blood." I scratched my forearm, and then my arm. I was gettin' the itches more and more around my injection sites lately.

"Her moms hit her safe for about fifty gees two weeks ago. Prior to that, she hit it for fifteen. Brat got tired of it. Knew her mother was smoking that rock. Long story short, on the night in question, Pesos and his niggas caught her slipping while coming out of her mother's crib and gave her an ultimatum. She could either lose her life or take theirs. Word on the street is she didn't hesitate. Her brother came home early from work, along with his daughters, and was added to the body count along with them. Hear no evil, see no evil, you feel me? Rules of the game." He took a strong pull from the cigarette and inhaled. "I can't believe you ain't know that."

I stood up, and one of my pistols fell from my hip. I bent over to pick it up, and School Boy upped two .44 Desert Eagles on me and cocked their hammers.

"Fuck you got on yo' mind, Blood? You planning on hating somethin' with them toolies? Huh?" he mugged me.

I picked my pistol up and put it on my waist. "Nigga, get yo' ass up. If I wanted to bam yo' ass, I'da did that awhile ago when you had your head down tooting that shit. Now, let's put this plan into motion. I'ma handle my end of things and get the fuck out of Chicago for good."

He lowered his guns and looked at me from the side of his face. "Yeah, awright." He took a seat on the couch and put his guns away. "You know you're the only nigga I've ever pulled a gun on that didn't flinch up like a li'l bitch? You got a lot of heart. That's why I fuck wit' you, Heinous. You live up to that muthafucking name. I got something to show you. You ever fuck wit' Walthers?"

He stood up and pulled the closet door open, shoved the clothes to the side, stuck his hand in, and came out of it wit' a briefcase. He set it on the table beside the lamp and clicked the latches on it, smiling the whole time. The wrinkles on the back of his head were more prominent than I remembered them being.

I shook my head. "What you talking about? A different kind of tech or something? If so, I probably have." I rubber-necked to see what he was about to unleash. I was still replaying what he'd told me about Brat over and over in my head. I was fucked up mentally more than I could say, but I couldn't let him know I was discombobulated. I didn't know how he would use that against me.

He shook his head. "Nall, Blood, not just any pistol. That shit too easy. I need you to make an example out of Lost Boy and my ex-bitch. Really make that shit gory so the whole city get to talking. I'ma be wit' the nigga right before she show up, so I can watch you do your thing in living, muthafucking color. That's how that shit gon' go." He opened the briefcase all the way and clapped his hands together. "Damn! Huh, check this out. Same kind James Bond uses, nigga!"

He handed my an eight-inch gun with a handle

that was gray and had grip indentations on it. I turned it over and over in my hand. It was real pretty. The light from the lamp caused it to gleam in the room. I nodded while holding it. "Aw, you on some Billy-The-Kid-type shit, huh?"

"Bing-muthafucking-o, my nigga." He laughed. "I want you to blast they bitch-ass. I'm talking do 'em so good they shut the city down and roll the tanks through this bitch. You remember we was the ones that made them do it before."

I nodded. "Hell yeah. We had to get them Crip niggas off the south side. I think I got four bodies under my belt that summer. It should've been more. Can't believe most of them niggas lived."

He shrugged his shoulders. "It happen like that sometimes. But it won't with these two, am I right?" He lowered his eyes and leaned into my face, running his tongue across his teeth. I pushed his ass back. "Damn, my nigga. I can hear you from over there. Get the fuck out my face. You smell like that bullshit."

He crushed the cigarette out in the ashtray and smile wickedly. "Let's just handle this bidness, Heinous. That way you can go your way and I can go mine. I can tell that us being in the same vicinity all the time isn't healthy. Males never get along. See what I'm saying?"

I sucked my teeth and looked him over. I imagined myself blowing his face off with both guns. I didn't like this fuck-boy. I couldn't wait to put him six feet under the dirt right after I used the same katana blades he'd given me to kill somebody else. "Yeah, I dig you, Blood. I couldn't have said it better."

***

My head was spinning like crazy all night. I kept trying to see where I'd went wrong with Brat. If she'd taken money to set me up, why hadn't I been able to see that in her character? I wondered if I was growing soft like mother was making it seem like I was. Had I turned bitch and lost that monster that dwelled deep in the pits of my soul? I didn't know.

I rubbed the alcohol pad over the skin of my inner bicep. I cringed as I saw all of the track marks in my arm already. Was I becoming a junkie? Was I no better than the average dope addict on the street? Had I lost myself? Would I see twenty-six years old? How was this game of death going to end? Would I be a survivor or a casualty?

I wrapped a belt around my arm when there was a beating on the door. It made me jump up and grab my pistol off the night stand. My clumsiness knocking the lamp off of the table and onto the floor. Now I was irritated. "Man, who the fuck is it," I picked the lamp up and saw in addition to knocking it off the stand, I'd spilled a nice portion of my work to the carpet. I knelt and began to scoop it back onto the saucer it had previously been on.

"Say, man, it's School Boy. Open this bitch up. It's urgent," he hollered through the door.

I took another minute before I answered the door with my gun. I didn't trust this nigga as far as I could throw him.

He brushed past me and into the room with his

face balled up. "That bitch pregnant by this fuck-nigga. I want that bitch dead tonight. Lost Boy out of town until Friday. We'll hit his ass when he get back. But I want her knocked off tonight, Blood."

I looked at this fool like he was crazy. "So you want me to kill this bitch because she pregnant? Why not wait until Lost Boy back in town and do this bidness then? That seem real suckerish to me."

I sat down, finished getting my work ready, and shot my dope into my system. My head was pounding, and I didn't feel like getting into a big thing with this big, goofy-ass nigga.

He hopped up and spilled ashes from his cigarette on the carpet. "I paid you a million up front, nigga. A million to do what the fuck I want you to do. You can't put no stipulations on my money. You gon' whack this bitch, and that's gon' be that. Let's go. She at home right now. Drunk, and out of it. I'm going to enjoy this kill. Bring yo' ass on."

I wanted to fill this nigga with slugs. Every fiber of my being told me to hit him up right then and there. The only problem was if I did that, then I would lose my in to Pesos and Lost Boy. I needed to smoke both of those fools in order to ensure the safety and stability of my family. As long as they had breath in their lungs, I had to worry about something happening to my beloveds. As much as I wanted to kill School Boy, I knew Pesos and Lost Boy's deaths were more important. School Boy would get what was coming to him. I was sure of that.

I nodded my head at this chump. "Awright, take me to where she is, and I'ma give you a show you'll never forget."

Hood Rich

With the heroin pumping through my system I meant every word of that.

***

School Boy took the key and placed it into the lock, then looked over his shoulder at me. "Look, bruh, I don't give no fuck about this bitch, as you can see. The bloodier you make this shit, the better. Everybody think I'm out of town in Miami, so this shit ain't gon' come back to me. Just do your thing. I'll take $500,000 off of that bill. You dig me?"

I situated the gorilla mask on my face and nodded. "Fuck all this talking. Let's go, nigga."

He opened the back door and slipped inside with me tailing him. When I came through the back door, I saw there were two sets of stairs: one leading to the second level of the house and the other leading into the basement. We took the ones leading to the second level of the house.

The hallway was pitch black, so much so I couldn't see where I was stepping. I used my ears to follow him. When we made it upstairs, there was another door he needed to open, and he did.

He stepped into the house, and I followed until he stopped and I bumped into the back of him and got irritated. He held out his big arm, stopping me. "There that bitch go, right there," he whispered, pointing into the dining room of their duplex.

Tanya, his baby mother, was sitting at the table with a bottle of Bombay in front of her and a half-glass of the liquor in her right hand. There was a blunt burning in the ashtray, and she had Ashanti's

Rescue playing out of the speakers in the crib.

She looked into the kitchen where the back door led us and scrunched her face. "School Boy, is that you? It's only Wednesday. I thought you wasn't getting home 'til Thursday?" She shook her head and cleared the glass of liquor, pouring herself another one.

Her hair was all over the place. She was caramel-skinned with a pretty face and banging body. I'd never seen her really up close, but I had from a distance, and all I could say was shorty was strapped. Chicago thick.

School Boy sucked his teeth. "Go in there and handle your bidness, bruh. Make that bitch feel what that blaster be about."

I opened my fatigue jacket, slid the gun out of it, and made my way into the living room with it in my right hand. School Boy walked in front of me, and I swear I had visions of grabbing him and bustin' him in the side of the head. What type of nigga killed his woman because she cheated on him with some other dude? He was a classic simp if you asked me. A sucker for love. I didn't like this punk at all.

When he stepped into the dining room with me behind him, Tanya's eyes got big. She looked down and saw the gun in my hand and the mask on my face, and it was like she knew what was about to happen. I expected her to run or scream, but she did none of that. She simply smiled and poured herself another shot of Bombay. "You finally got somebody to kill me, huh, School Boy? I been waiting on this day for a few months. You took long enough." She smiled, and drank from the glass

School Boy took a seat across from her and interlocked his fingers. "It's time to pay the piper, bitch. You been fucking off on me long enough. Everything has an end, even you. Handle this bitch, Blood."

She held up one finger as I made my way around the table toward her, stopping me in place. I don't know why I stopped, but I did.

She grabbed the bottle of Bombay and drained it, then slammed it on the table. "Before I die, nigga, I just want you to know I hate you. I been miserable ever since yo' li'l dick-ass diseases that you gave me from sleeping around with these thots of Chicago. I don't think you've ever been faithful to me, and now you're mad because I'm fucking Lost Boy and pregnant with his kid? Why? You don't even take care of the ones you got. Mad because I won't take yo' trifling-ass off of Child Support? Fuck you, School Boy. I'd rather die than to be bound by your bum-ass for life. Do what the fuck you gotta do, you and this gorilla." She held up two middle fingers, and I could tell she was pissed off and wasted. "I fucked your brother, too. How you like them apples?"

"Aw!" School Boy snapped and threw the glass table out of the way. He rushed her and knocked her out of the chair with one vicious blow. She flew backward into the wall and slid to the carpet.

He was on her ass. "I'm sick of you, bitch. You fucked my brother and my right-hand man?"

He tightened his hands around her neck, squeezing so hard a thick vein appeared in her forehead. She kicked her legs wildly. Her eyes bulged out of her face.

"Die, bitch! Die! Aw!" he hollered, slobber dripping from the corners of his mouth.

I raised the gun and pulled the trigger, bustin' it at the top of his skull. *Bam!* But my angle was off. The bullet entered his skull at a shallow angle, blasting a hole in his temple on its way out, but not killin' him.

Instead of dying instantly, School Boy stood up with blood oozing down his face. "Uh. Uh. Uh." Both of his arms reached out for me. His eyes were bucked.

I sidestepped him and backhanded him across the face. A thick slit formed, and more blood spilled out of him. "Sucka-ass nigga, you want me to kill this bitch when you not done?" I hit him with the butt of the gun again, then kicked him in the groin as hard as I could.

Tanya ran and balled up in a corner of the dining rom, strugglin' to breathe. She choked on her spit and rubbed her neck.

School Boy fell to his knees. From the neck up he was all bloody. I could tell he was fighting for his life. His mouth opened. He tried to make it back to his feet, groaning.

I grabbed the bottle of Bombay and crashed it on the back of his head. There was so much blood that some popped into the air and onto my gorilla mask. I didn't give a fuck. I swung the broken bottle, sticking it into his neck. I pulled it out and kicked him in the chest, knocking him to the floor.

He struggled to get up from a push-up position. He fell face-first.

I kicked him onto his back. "Nigga, don't you

73

ever follow my bitch or come to where I lay my head at. I fear no man. Don't no nigga call shots over me. Bar none, bitch-nigga. Bar muthafucking none!"

I took the bottle and slammed it into the upper portion of his neck that connected to the back of his head and left it there as I stood up. "Bitch-ass nigga. Blood in, Blood out."

Tanya looked terrified. She pissed herself and kept trying to back further and further away from me. Tears ran down her cheeks.

"Hey, shorty, chill! You ain't got shit to worry about. This nigga hired me to kill you, but I don't get down like that. I crush niggas, not hos. Unless I have to. Live your life and have a happy pregnancy. Fuck this nigga. Help me get his body downstairs so I can get rid of it, and you clean up this mess."

She jumped up with her knees wobbling and helped me do exactly that. When we finally got his body downstairs and into the trunk of the Chevy Caprice Classic we'd rolled in for Tanya's murder, she grabbed my arm and kissed the back of my glove.

"Thank you. Thank you so much. I swear I ain't gon' say shit to nobody. I'ma go up there and clean up this mess and act like this never happened. That's on my kids. He got two million in cash upstairs. You can have it. You saved my life. I swear you can have every penny of it." She hugged me and took a step back with tears in her eyes.

It was three in the morning and dark in the their house. Bugs were everywhere, and I was ready to dump this fool's body and get back to Milwaukee. "Shorty, how many kids do you have?" I asked, feeling tempted by the money. Two million was a whole lot of cash.

"Two girls, and one child on the way." She hugged herself because of the cold. I could see her teeth chattering.

"Take that money and be smart with it. Give your baby a better life. Quit fucking wit' these low-life bitch-niggas. They gon' keep you pregnant and dependent. You hear me? Fuck this nigga and Lost Boy. Both of them are trifling."

She stuttered. "I-I-I don't want to be with him. He forces me. I hate his guts. What if you took the money and got rid of him for me so I can live my life somewhere else? He say if I mess with any other man, he gon' kill me, too. I don't know what to do." She rubbed the sides of her arms and danced in place to stay warm.

I looked her over closely. "Wait a minute, you ain't fucking wit' Blood like that, either?" I got excited.

She backed away and held her hands up. I took ahold of her wrist and pulled her to me. I know it must've been scary for her with me towering over her in a gorilla mask, but it was what it was. "Look, shorty, I don't give a fuck about Lost Boy. So if you want me to knock him off, then I'll need more info."

She looked like she was ready to burst into tears. "Oh my God, I'll give you so much more than that."

Hood Rich

Chapter 7

I chose to lay back for a full three weeks after I knocked School Boy off. I just needed to regroup. My head was fucked up on so many levels, so instead of being in Chicago, I decided to chill with my queens out in Milwaukee. I felt like needed to be around those that loved me because I was losing myself.

The heroin was taking more and more of a hold on me. I was up to shooting the poison into my system about seven times a day, sometimes more depending on the evil daydreams I had while nodding. I kept seeing the Angel of Death every time I closed my eyes long enough to doze off, and that was freaking me out. Not to the point I was scared of it, but I felt my impending death was very close. I just didn't know how close. I wasn't ready to die, but at the same time I didn't fear death, either. I knew it was a natural thing that had to happen.

Three weeks after I murdered School Boy, I decided I was just going to live life to the fullest and treat every day as if it was my last, which was why I was using so heavily. One afternoon in the third week after I iced School Boy, I was sitting in the living room watching the Lakers and NBA game, hoping LeBron would drop forty on they ass, when Leah came into the living room in some real little booty shorts and a small tank top that exposed the fact she wasn't wearing a bra over her breasts.

She came and slid into my lap and kissed my cheek with a smile on her pretty face. "I love you so much, Jahrome, do you know that?" she asked, blocking the television with her big head. She smelled like Burberry perfume.

"I looked around her head and to the big screened television just as LeBron dunked the ball in Kevin Durant's face and hollered, then started beating his chest. "What you want, Leah? You gotta be up to something. You're being way too nice." I looked into her eyes and raised my right eyebrow. "What's good?"

She shrugged her shoulders. "Dang, why I just can't tell you I love you without you thinking I'm up to something?"

She avoided eye contact with me, and that was a pure telltale sign she was up to something. She also fidgeted in my lap.

"Because I been knowing and spoiling you ever since you learned how to walk. I know you're up to something, so you might as well spit that shit out." I laughed and continued to watch the basketball game. I was still high as fuck. I was thinking about getting her off my lap because the drug took my penis' conscience away. She was way too thick to be sitting there, anyway.

She sighed and turned sideways, putting her arm around my neck. She laid her face in the crux of it and kissed it with her soft lips right along the thick vein there.

I shuddered and really needed to get her off of my lap. My piece stood right up, poking her. I was sure of that. I tried to move her off of my lap. "Get up, Leah, fo' real. My dick is hard as hell. You shouldn't be sitting on my lap. I'm fucked up right now."

I tried to push her away. She held me tighter and situated herself so her thighs had trapped my piece. She placed her face back into the crux of my neck, and kissed it. "You act like that's the first time I done felt you rise. I ain't studding that." She kissed me again. "Big bruh, I need a car. I'm tired of calling Ubers and using this city's public transportation system. You havin' all this money, ain't no way I should be on a fucking bus. Don't you love me?" She rocked just a bit.

Tingles shot up from my basement and caused my heart to beat hard in my chest. I reached between us and pulled my piece so it lay against my stomach. The pressure her body was applying to it was too much for me. I didn't give a fuck how horny I got, I couldn't see myself smashing Leah. That would have been way over the line. I didn't think we would ever come back from that. She was already too clingy, but it didn't really bother me. We had been through a lot, so I understood.

She turned her back to me and scooted backward, pushing my dick into my stomach. "Mm, don't be tryna hide that big 'ol thang." She looked back at me, sucking her bottom lip as her eyes lowered. Her face was flushed, and I knew what time it was. This was very dangerous.

I grabbed her by her hips and made her stand up. Her panties were all in her booty, so far that both cheeks were exposed. She turned around to face me with a look of confusion. Her nipples threatened to poke holes in her skimpy tank top. Below, her camel toe was on full display.

"Dang, why you make me get up?" she asked,

running her hand over her flat stomach.

I shook my head and took a deep breath. "'Cause, shorty, you got me hard as hell. You gotta chill. Fuck." I looked her over and couldn't believe how bad she'd gotten. I knew I wasn't supposed to pay attention to that, but like I said, that heroine took my penis' conscience away. Had she been any other female, I would have bent her ass over that couch and fucked her for a few hours. Outside of Yani, Leah was the baddest female I had ever seen in the physical.

"What kind of car are you trying to get, Leah?"

She squealed and ran out of the room. When she came back, she was holding her phone in her left hand. "I want this 2019 Benz truck. I'll take care of it and keep it up. There won't ever be any problems with it, I swear, and if there is, I'll take care of it. I promise, Jahrome."

I frowned. "Leah, you ain't gotta say all that shit. You know I got you. G'on, get dressed so we can cop it right now. I need to relieve some of this pressure, I'll be right back.

She trailed her eyes down to my piece, and smiled. "You sure you don't want me to help? I mean, come on, who really cares? How close have we been to doing something, anyway?" She stepped up to me and grabbed it, squeezing it in her hand.

I smacked her hand away. "Go get dressed. I'm good. Just meet me back here in, like, an hour. I should be ready then."

She kissed my cheek, and shrugged her shoulders. "Okay, well, I'll do that, then." She walked out of the living room with her panties still in her ass. All I could do was shake my head.

I rushed out of there and into my bedroom. When I got inside it, Yani was lying in the bed, sleeping with he right knee up against her rib cage. She wore a blue G-string that barely hid any part of her nakedness.

I got undressed right at the foot of the bed, and crawled across it. I opened her booty cheeks and stuck my face right in between them, licking around her small anus before sucking her lips into my mouth from the back.

"Mm, Daddy. What are you doing back there?" She arched her back and placed her right hand on her ass, holding the cheeks apart for me. She had a big ass, just like Leah. It was hot and fleshy. The only difference was she was a little lighter than Leah, and I could do whatever I wanted to do to her.

I licked up and down her gap and slid my tongue between her lips, tasting her cat. My hands rubbed all over her ass, squeezing it. "Baby, I wanna fuck this pussy. You can just relax. I'll do everything. I know you're still tired."

See, me and Yani had been fucking three and four times a day for nearly a month straight. I couldn't get enough of that pussy. Every time I thought I was through, my dick would get hard again, and then I was back between them legs again, going to work. Before I'd went into the living room to watch the game, we'd just gotten out of the shower after fucking for two hours straight.

She climbed to her knees and laid the palms of her hands on the bed, sticking her ass up in the air and spreading her thighs. "This pussy is yours,

Daddy. You already know that. And I want it. Go ahead, fuck yo' baby. I want it, too." She rested her cheek on top of the covers.

I kissed her right on her pussy hole and sucked her as if it was a nipple. Her juices started to run out of her and drip off of my chin. I got behind her and slid my big helmet into her hot pocket, feeling the warmth engulf me. Eagerly, I moaned into my throat and dived all the way in with a greasy dick and slammed it home. Took ahold of her waist and got to working that pussy. Her breasts bounced up and down on her chest like two water balloons with thick nipples on the ends of them. Her face was all balled up, her mouth wide open and breathing heavily. The headboard knocked into the wall. "Un. Un. Un. Fuck. You love this pussy. You love this pussy. Don't you?" she gasped, rocking back into me.

I had my eyes closed tightly, trying to get the image of what I'd just seen and felt in the living room out of my head. "Yeah, baby. Yeah, Daddy love this pussy. I love it. Aw shit, I do." I got to fucking her as hard as I could, long-stroking her for all she was worth, busting that pussy wide open.

I felt a presence behind me. Then hands rubbed all over my back. "Fuck her, Jahrome. Make that bitch take all that dick. She can't handle it. Look at her face."

Leah knelt beside Yani wit her ass in the air. She'd taken her panties off. She spread her knees, exposing her glistening pussy. The lips were slightly opened, as if her finger had just been in there, playing around or something. She slid her hand under her stomach and opened the sex lips wide, displaying her pink.

I had to close my eyes as tight as I could to avoid looking at it. I got to tearing Yani's ass up, fucking her so hard and deep that she wound up grabbing a pillow and smashing her face into it, screaming at the top of her lungs. She beat on the bed with her fist as she took her assault.

Leah sat beside her and fingered herself. Occasionally she would kiss Yani's lips or suck her distended nipples, but for the most part she sat with her back against the headboard, pleasuring herself until she came back-to-back, never taking her eyes away from Yani and my connected sex parts.

Finally, the feeling became too much. Yani slammed back into me and came hard, drenching my lap with her juices. I felt her walls slurping at me and came deep within her channel before slipping out of her and lying on my back. As soon as I landed, she sucked her juice off of me and pumped my dick in her fist. "You be fucking the shit out of me wit' this big-ass baseball bat. Uh!" She opened her thighs wide and closed them, then passed out with her big booty in the air.

***

Four hours later, at about 3 o'clock in the afternoon, Leah drove off of the lot in a 2019 black and platinum Mercedes Benz truck. The salesman was one hunnit. He let me pay for her truck with cold, hard cash. I liked that, and I told him I would be fucking with him in the very near future. I wound up dropping $35,000 for her truck and hitting him with an additional five bands just so he would let me pay cash. All in all, my sister had cost me forty thousand dollar in a matter of hours, and I felt like she deserved every penny of it. I sat back in her passenger seat and lowered the window just a tad. It was September, and there was a nice breeze coming. Life, for the moment, wasn't bothering me. The heroine was calling, but that was it. I knew I'd answer that phone call real soon.

"You know something, Jahrome? You always make sure I'm good, ever since I could remember. I love the hell out of you." She waited until she pulled up at a stop light, leaned over, and kissed my cheek, leaving a light pink lip print on my cheek from her M.A.C. lipstick.

I had a Mach .11 on my lap and was looking from one side of the street to the next. Even though I was in Milwaukee, my eyes were peeled. The fool School Boy had located me once. There was no telling who he'd told about my whereabouts or who could have possibly been following us, so I was ready to go.

"You know I got you, li'l sis. We gon' put you a system in here and slap some rims on this bad boy, if you want me to. Gotta have you shining hard. You're my sister." I was proud of that, so thankful she was alive. That bullet could have easily taken her life, and then I wouldn't have had a sister. That would have devastated me. She was my heart and soul, and she had been ever since we were little kids.

She shook her head. "I don't need all of that. Just the fact you were able to cop this for me, and you're here, alive and well, that's enough for me. I'm a very simple girl, and I'm crazy about you. Dang. I sound like I'm just seven years old." She rolled her eyes and pulled away from the lights. "You wanna go dancing or something? Like, let's just spend the rest of the day together. It's been a while since we've –"

Bam!

There was loud sound of crunching metal as a black Navigator slammed into her driver's side, knocking her into my lap. Her head flew into the passenger's side windshield and went through it. I could hear her screaming.

Our truck spun in circles and eventually hit a light pole, knocking Leah back into the truck and into the back seat. My head slammed into the dashboard. The airbag deploy, throwing me backward.

The Navigator slammed on its brakes, and two dudes got out with fully-automatics in their hands. They took off running toward our truck with masks covering half of their faces.

I dove for the floor and grabbed my Mach. 11. Before I could wrap my fingers all the way around the handle, Leah jumped up with her hand pressed to the gash in her head. Blood ran down the side of her face.

"Jahrome. Jahrome. It hurts, big bruh. It hurts."

The two figures stepped to the side of the truck and began to shoot.

The first shots went into the back of my sister's head and out of her face, splattering me with its contents. "No!" I hollered as she fell on top of me.

I raised my Mach and started shooting wildly. *Boom. Boom. Boom.* The fire spit from the barrel in their direction, shattering the windows. They returned fire briefly, then took off running, jumped

Hood Rich

into the Navigator, and sped away.

I looked down at the truck's plates and saw they read Illinois.

Leah was unmoving on the floor of the truck. Half of her head was blown completely off. There was a strong stench of death rising from her body. My face and midsection were covering in her brain matter.

I put the Mach to my head and squeezed the trigger. Nothing.

"Ah! Ah! My muthafucking sister! Leah, no! Please, God, no!" I hollered.

I squeezed and squeezed the trigger, but it wouldn't go off. I smacked it on the side and tried to re-cock it, then pulled the trigger again. Still nothing.

Finally, I threw it at a door in the back, gathered up what was left of my sister, and held her until the police showed up. They found her bled out with me sitting in a puddle of her blood, tears streaming down my face.

Chapter 8

They kept me in the police station for two full weeks. The shit was so bogus that I missed my sister's funeral. The entire time, I didn't eat more than a bite of food a day. I ate just enough so I didn't pass out. On top of losing her and all the bullshit Milwaukee had going on in their county jail, I was going through some crazy withdrawals after the first day of my arrest. My stomach felt like it was turned inside out. I was shitting every five minutes, then I'd have to turn around and throw up where I'd just shit. I got the shivers, and everything made me nauseous. I was busting out in cold sweats, and my head felt like it was being smashed in by a sledge hammer.

I cried all day and night long over missing Leah. I couldn't believe she was gone. I made Yani and my mother get the fuck out of the house as soon as I got ahold of a phone, and no more than ten minutes after they pulled away Yani said the house was riddled with more than a thousand bullets and set ablaze. The war had spilled over from Chicago into Milwaukee.

***

On the fourteenth day of my stay in the Milwaukee jail, Taylor showed up to the interrogation room with a grin on his ugly face. He slapped a bunch of files in front of me and pulled out a cigarette.

I was so cold that I was shaking as if I was sitting naked in the snow. I was fien'ing for a fix and probably would have done anything for one.

87

"Well, you thought if you ran away from Chicago, all of the drama would just leave you, huh?" He laughed and lit the end of his smoke. "You want one?"

I was shivering like crazy, hugging myself. "Hell nall. I don't fuck wit' them cancer sticks." My teeth chattered together.

"Cancer should be the last thing you're worried about. I can guarantee one of them niggas from the Windy gon' kill you long before any cancer will. You can bet everything you own on that."

"Yeah, well, still. I'm good." I continued to shake like crazy.

"Perhaps that ain't strong enough. Maybe you need something like this." He took a syringe filled with a liquid substance out of his coat pocket and sat it on the table. "It's only sixty percent, but I know sixty is better than no percent You want it?" He looked me in the eyes and slowly smiled, guessing that he had the upper hand. And he did.

I didn't know if he was serious or not, so I grabbed the syringe with lighting speed and ran to the corner of the interrogation room and sat on the floor. I held my arm out and found a vein, praying he wasn't on his way to stopping me. A soon as I located a thick one, I jammed the needle into me and fed the poison into my system. My eyelids fluttered. I came on myself and shivered. My toes curled. "Fuck, that's good."

Taylor stood up and frowned. "Bring yo' ass over here. Now we need to talk on some serious shit." He took his seat and set up his laptop.

The metal stool felt like little knives in my ass.

Fuck, the dope might have been weak, but it was better than nothing. At least my sick had left for the time being. That was all that mattered to me. My dick was still hard in my county oranges. I felt awkward being in front of a man in that state.

"First of all, I'm sorry for your loss. Unfortunately, things are only going to get worst. Pesos done stepped up his game. He's now linked up with the Malo Noche Cartel out of Mexico. They are one of the deadliest groups of sons of bitches you'll ever deal with. Trust me on this. Their sole purpose is to divide, kill, conquer, and get as rich as they can off the backs of those they force under their wing. Pesos' crew generates about two million dollars a day out there in the Wild Hundreds. It was only a matter of time before one of these organizations stepped in and took ownership of him and his crew. You see, in the drug game, everybody owns somebody. There's no such thing as free enterprise. The higher up you go, the deadlier things get. Nobody really wants to be that connected to the plug because you can lose your life."

I scratched my arm and closed my eyes, still trying to enjoy my high, hoping it lasted longer than twenty or thirty minutes. "What that got to do with me, man? I ain't fucking around in yo' punk-ass city no more. The war should eventually end. When I get out of here, I'm going either east or south. Fuck Chicago!" I didn't mean that shit at all. I wasn't going to let these niggas get away with killing my sister. I didn't care if I lost my life in the process, I was coming for their asses.

"Oh, hell nall, you got the game fucked up. Not

Hood Rich

only are you coming back to Chicago, but you're going to kill Pesos. Because of you, he's a threat to the city. A threat we can't gamble on. The only way for us to reclaim the Hundreds is if he's dead, and you're going to do it, or you're going down for every last one of these murders in this file. And trust me, I can make them all stick because yo' dumbass left a part of you at every crime scene. Something even you couldn't wipe way."

He broke into a bout of laughter that irritated my soul. I was trying to think about every murder I'd ever committed. It had been instilled in me by the streets at a young age to never leave evidence. "Nigga, fuck you. I'm calling your bluff. I don't know what you got, but I know for a fact I always wiped down afterwards. That in them files, but it ain't got nothing to do with me."

"Boy, shut up. You got to be one of the stupidest niggas I have ever ran into in Chicago. Don't you know that our city is one of the most heavily-surveilled cities in America? You can't do shit without Big Brother catching you doin' it. Not only have you left your DNA at every crime scene in Chicago, but there is also footage of yo' stupid-ass fleeing each scene. The one that shocked me the most was this one." He turned his laptop computer around and pressed the arrow for PLAY. I squinted at the screen. As soon as there were shots, the screen went from black to live in an infrared setting. It scanned up and down Brat's block, and then zoomed in on her residence. At the bottom of the screen it said, "Gunshots detected at 8675 South LaSalle." Then it zoomed in on her crib. I set back in my seat, nervous,

90

then leaned forward again. There I was three minutes later, leaving the house with the pillowcase in my hand. It showed me getting into my truck and pulling away. The camera zoomed in on the license plates. After it was read, the screen flipped to green, and my mug shot popped up. Under it, my entire record. I was mortified. I couldn't breathe. I just knew I was about to serve life in prison. Taylor had me by the balls. I started to sweat, my high leaving me.

"Every time a shot is fired in my city, a signal goes off and comes directly to the nearest police station. That activates a camera in the area, and the system estimates where in particular the shot came from. It is more than ninety five percent accurate. But, in your case, it was a hundred percent, and has been for a while now. So, why'd you kill Brat? I thought you –"

"I don't want to talk about none of that shit."

"What do you want, ace boon coon?" He popped a stick of gum into his mouth. "I'm listening." He locked his fingers behind his head and kicked his feet up on the table.

"What do you want me to do? How can I make this shit go away?" I asked, sweating profusely. I couldn't believe that system. I got to thinking about all types of shit I'd done, and there was a lot. I'd shot my first person when I was only eleven years old, and five more that same summer. I was wondering if all of those shooting were in that big file he had in front of him.

"I want you to finish what you started. I want you to kill Pesos. Not only that, but I'm going to help you with a little bit of information." He pinched his nose and sniffed loudly. "Like I said before, I don't make more than $60,000. It will be up to you to hit him when the picking will be good and plenty. The only thing is I want all the money. I don't want the feds to step in and take him off the streets. That could ruin everything. You gotta do this shit within the next two weeks. If you don't, you're going down for a really long time, Jahrome." He laughed. "Between the two of you, I think you're more dangerous to have roaming. You've got more connections around outside of a prison, but he's more mean, more murder, more money, more power, and more innocent people at stake. He has to go. It's as simple as that."

He pulled a thin file out of his briefcase. "You walk out of these doors tonight, this file will be with your belongings. Study it and formulate your plan of action. You got two weeks to slay this beast. Either you slay him, or I slay you. It's as simple as that. I don't give a fuck either way. Both of you are filthy niggas, and when it's all said and done, you're going to reap what you've sown." He mugged me and got up. "I'll be in touch. Don't get too comfortable, Heinous. Go take care of your mother."

***

I was released at ten o'clock that night. When I stepped out of the doors, it was snowing like crazy. Yani was parked at the curb in front of the county jail in her pink Lexus truck. When she saw me, she opened the driver's door to me with smoke from the cold coming out of her mouth.

I opened my arms wide and picked her up into the air as soon as she crashed into me. It felt so good to have her in my arms again. "Baby. Damn, you feel so good. I've missed you," I said, hugging her like my life depended on it.

She was crying. "Daddy, I'm so sorry about Leah. I'm so sorry I know that kilt you. I wish it would have been me. I know you're hurting," she sobbed, holding me tight. "I've missed you so much."

I picked her up, and she wrapped her legs around me. The snow continued to fall from the sky. I was freezing, but that didn't matter. She mattered. I was falling in love with her all over again. I felt like she was all I had left in this world. "Baby, stop talking crazy like that. I need you. Yeah, we lost Leah, but losing you would have been just as rough. You're my heart just as much as she was."

I put her down and kissed her soft lips, holding the sides of her beautiful face. Her lips were cold at first, but then they warmed up, and so did my body. She smelled like Chanel. I was intoxicated by the feminine scent of her.

She broke our kiss and rubbed her thumb over my lips. "Come on. Let's get you home and out of this cold. I need you to just hold me for the night. I've been missing it more than anything else. I mean, I know you wanna get in between my thighs, but please, when we're done with that, just hold me."

I nodded and opened the driver's door for her to get inside of the truck, then walked around it and got in myself. It felt like I'd been locked down for years. I was so happy to be out, even though I knew I had a major war ahead of me.

***

While I was away, Yani had taken it upon herself to rent out a room in the Radisson Hotel, the one that was located in Waukegan, Illinois, right outside of Gurney Mills. I was a nice, clean hotel, and right in the business district. There were police cars everywhere I looked, and security guards walking all throughout the hotel and even up and down the street the hotel was located on. The area where the Radisson was located was familiar with lots of tourists who navigated from the Six Flags Great America about ten miles or so up the highway.

Even though I didn't fuck with the police, I figured for at least the time being, their presence was necessary. I couldn't see any of my enemies getting to me while I was at this place. Their presence also meant my mother and Yani would also be good. And for me, that was more important than my own safety and security.

We got to our room, and Yani stopped outside of the door with the keycard in her hand. She turned around, stood on her tippy-toes, and kissed my lips. "I'm so glad you're out of there. I was going crazy out here without you." She smiled and slid the card into the lock, opening the door.

It was a standard hotel room. A big bed in the middle of it with a gray blanket covering it. A lamp on each side of it, held up by nightstands. There was a bathroom, a balcony, a closet for our things, a big screen television, and that was it. But it was all I needed until I could get my mind right.

I brushed right past her, and into the bathroom. I needed to shower, needed to get that jail shit up off of me. It's like a man never really felt free until he was able to get the stink of the incarceration off of him, so that as my first priority.

I dropped my clothes to the ground and set the water temperature. I tested it with my hand, and then got inside. The water cascaded into my face. I closed my eyes and opened my mouth to get a mouthful of the free water, then spit it back into the drain.

The shower curtain was pulled back. I didn't even open my eyes because I knew who it was. I felt Yani's soft breasts press into my back, the nipples already spiked. She slid her hand around my waist and grabbed ahold of my piece, squeezing it. I closed my eyes tighter.

"Mm, damn, baby. That feel so good." When I turned around to face her, she dropped to her knees and sucked me into her mouth, giving me some of the best head I'd had in a long time. Her slurping noises drown out by the water in the shower.

"You love it, Daddy?" She licked around the head and began to spear her head on it like a pro. Her titties jiggled under her. She had her eyes shut tight because the water was splashing right into her face.

I rested my back against the shower wall, her hair tangled in my fingers. I was breathing heavy and on the verge of giving her a mouthful. One thing about Yani was she was a beast when it came to sucking me off and getting me right. I loved her head game.

"Yeah, boo. Suck that dick for Daddy. Suck it."

She moaned around it and sped up her pace. She

popped it out long enough to say, "Cum in my mouth. Your baby wanna taste you. Please." She sucked me back in and got to going crazy over my head wit' no hands.

My toes curled, and then I opened my mouth wide and let out a groan that came from deep in my belly. The next thing I knew, I was splashing down her throat and she was swallowing all of my seed and still sucking.

She pumped it a few more times in her hand and stood up, bending over. "Daddy, how you want it? You want this pussy from the back, or do you wanna fuck me up?" She was excited. Her hand rubbed up and down her ass. Her asshole winking at me.

I kissed her cheeks and ran my tongue in circles around it. "Damn, boo. I be forgetting how thick yo' li'l ass is. That's why I'm always hitting this shit from the back, though. How could I put something this thick on its back? Fuck that."

I pressed my head in between her pussy lips and slid him in. Her pussy separated and accepted me. My pipe slid all the way into her body and disappear, then I pulled back and saw I was saturated with her juices. She felt nice and hot. Her pussy was tight from the time she'd gone without sex, waiting on me.

She placed both of her hands on the tiled wall, and pushed backward to accept as much of my dick as she possibly could. " Aw, shit! Fuck me! Fuck me! Fuck me! Fuck me! Yes! Yes! I missed you! I missed you! Heinous!"

She was throwing that ass back at me like a monster. It crashed into my lap and wobbled on her frame. I smacked it and continued to ride that big-ass booty, long-stroking her hot pocket and loving every minute of it.

There wasn't nothing like pussy when a nigga was fresh out. Nothing. Yani had that snap, too. That shit that wrapped around a dick and didn't want to let it go. Her muscles were strong, yet silky. I grabbed ahold of her waist and watched my pipe dig into her, not knowing how much longer I was going to be able to last. I smacked her ass hard.

"Uh! Daddy. I'm finna cum. I'm finna cum. Smack it one more time and I'ma cum all over this fat-ass dick. Please!" She pulled forward and tooted her ass in the air, waiting in anticipation. I held my hand up high, and brought it down on that wet ass.

She yelped and screamed, then slammed back into me. "Again! Smack my ass again. Aw, fuck! Keep working it like that!" She popped her back and rolled it up.

Her kitty pulled and released me, keeping me on the brink of exploding. I got to fucking her like a savage, pulling her hair with one hand and smacking her ass with the other. Her cheeks continued to jiggle and shake. She was so thick. Damn, she had a cold-ass body.

Smack! "Aw, I'm cumming, Daddy. Oh, shit. I'm cumming so hard!" She fell against the wall face-first, cumming in thick rivers.

I crashed into her, still fucking her. Holding her waist with my feet spaced apart, I kept hitting her deepest regions until the feeling became too much. I couldn't take it no more. My dick got sensitive, and then my entire body locked up. The only thing I was able to move were my hips. Stabbing and stabbing.

"Aw, baby. I'm cumming. Daddy cumming in this pussy! Damn, it's so good," I growled and got to shooting her womb up.

***

After the shower, Yani, snuggled up to me, and rubbed my chest. Seemingly out of nowhere, she said, "I think we should up and leave this part of the country altogether. Wouldn't that be smart?" She looked up at me and rubbed the side of my face that needed to be shaved.

I hadn't had time to look over the files Taylor had given me. My body was sick. I needed a fix. The watered-down heroin Taylor had given me had worn off way before Yani came to pick me up, and even though I had been physically miserable up until the time she stepped in the shower with me, I tried my best to not let her know it. I missed her and knew I had to figure out our next move.

I kissed her forehead and sighed. "That's what I was thinking, baby. But it's not going to be so simple as that. You know that detective that showed up the two times I got shot up?" I asked, looking down at her.

She nodded. "Yeah, I do. What about him?"

"Dude got some serious dirt on me, boo. Dirt that'd put me away for the rest of my life. I'm talking murders and all kinds of shit. So, I'm stuck." I exhaled again, feeling sicker than I was five minutes ago. I needed a fix.

She sat all the way up, and looked down on me. Her perky, big breasts wobbled on her chest. She looked sexy.

"So, what is he going to do? Is he looking to lock you up or something? Because if that's the case, then we need to get the hell out of here. Like, tonight. I don't care where we have to go. I'm rolling with you. Look." She jumped out of the bed and pulled a big suitcase out of the closet, plopped it onto the bed, and opened it to reveal it was stuffed with bundles and bundles of cash. "This is all the money you had tucked away in your safe, plus the five hundred thousand I got for hocking the businesses to Hijeb, the Arab man who owns all of the property of western Chicago. I know you didn't tell me to do it, but I felt like taking the initiative. That's what good women do. So, this is 2.6 million dollars altogether. I know it's not a lot, but it's a start. Let's get the fuck out of here. Please."

Hood Rich

Chapter 9

My body felt like it was closing in on itself. I was so happy at how my woman had gotten down, but I couldn't focus. Fien'ing for the drug wouldn't allow me to. I needed order to make some sense out of our lives.

I started scratching myself real bad before I hopped out of bed in shivers. "Look, boo, let me go check on my mother right quick, and then we can figure out what we're going to do. I'm so thankful for you, though. Can't no woman hold me do n like you do, baby. I owe you the world, and as soon as I get this shit figured out, that's what I'ma render unto you. That's my word."

She stood at a distance, watching me get dressed with an angry mug on her face. "What is wrong with you?" She started across the room.

I was already dressed with boxers, my beater, and Jordans on my feet. I felt that was all I needed. I had to go shoot up. My body was calling for it. I was on the verge of screaming. I could barely think straight.

"Nothing, boo, I'm good. Just put the money back in the closet. I'll be right back. I just gotta go and check on her. Something ain't right. I can feel it." I scratched my inner forearm and passed gas. My system was giving up on me. I had to supply it with the gift of heroin. I just had to.

"Hurry yo' ass back here so we can figure this shit out. I don't feel safe, Heinous. We need to get the fuck up out of here, and soon, or we're all going to be dead. Please listen to me. I know what I'm talking about. Call it a woman's intuition." She sat on the bed and ran her hand through all of the money.

"Alright, baby. I'll be right back. I love you. I mean that."

"I love you, too, Jahrome. Now, hurry up. Please."

I slipped out of the room and into the hallway. Moving to my mother's door, I inserted the keycard. The door clicked loudly and then opened. Just as soon as it did, a horrible stench wafted out of the room. I pinched my nostrils and gagged from the strong odor that smelled like fish, musk, ass, and spoiled milk. It was like somebody had left a garbage can full of rotten products out in the sun for a week straight. It was baffling.

I nudged the door open and frowned, looking inside the room cautiously. "Mama, where you at? Why it stink so bad in here?" On top of it smelling like death's ass, the room was very hot, as if she had the heat set on 'roast.' I started sweating.

My mother wheeled her wheelchair across the floor, then hopped out of it and into the bed she'd been sleeping in. She as butt-naked, with her hair all over the place. All of the lights were off in the room. She had the blinds pulled down to prevent any sunlight from coming in, and two candles were burning. She ran her fingers through her unkempt hair and licked her white lips.

The further I got into the room, the stronger the odor became. It was so bad I could taste it at this point. I didn't know whether to breathe through my nose or mouth. Both had consequences that were unbearable.

"I just got out of jail, and I wanted to come and

see if you were good. I guess you ain't missed me at all, huh?"

"We buried your sister in Chicago right next to your father. I got her obituary in my purse, if you wanna see it. It was a nice service, not that many people came out. We didn't tell many either, though. Was afraid of what your enemies might do. But, yeah, she's gone now. My only daughter gone, like she never happened. Hopefully your father is going to take care of her. He was crazy about Leah. His joy is her." She scratched the bush between her legs.

"Nall, Ma. I don't want to see her like that. I want to keep all of the happy memories I have of her in my head. I can't stand to see her on some death paper. Screw that." I got the shivers. My stomach began to cramp real bad. "Mama, you got some medicine with you? I swear, I feel like my insides are being turned inside out."

She shook her head. "Nope. I only got me enough to last for the rest of the day. I don't feel like sending Yani back out there to find me some more. I don't think she can strike gold twice." She smacked her lips and laid on her side. There was a big sweat spot where she'd peeled her body away from the sheet.

I was itching like crazy and about to throw up. "Momma, how much you got, man? Damn. I'll go find some more. You ain't gotta hold it to your chest. I wouldn't do you like that."

"Jahrome, get yo' ass out of my room. Now. I ain't got enough to share, and that's just that. You got two good-ass legs on your body. Go find your own. Now, g'on, get! I'm not gon' say it again." She pointed toward the door.

Hood Rich

A sharp pain shot through my stomach. I fell to my knees. My head began to pound so bad that my nose bled. There was a high-pitched screeching in my ears. I felt like I was being tortured.

"Mama, please, don't do this to me. All I need is a taste to get me strong enough so I can go out and find what I need. I'll make sure I get enough for you, too. I'll buy a whole ounce just for you. That's twenty-eight grams of bliss. You hear me?" I dug my nails into my arm and scratched as hard a I could until bloody streaks occurred. Then my neck was itching, and my back. I was going crazy.

She reached under her pillow and held up a small Ziploc bag with a corner of China White heroin inside of it. "This is all I got left. It's getting to the point that if I don' take this heroin every three hours, I want to kill myself. I'm so close, Jahrome, that you have no idea. I've lost my daughter, my dignity, and my leg. Now, this dope is all I have left. I aunt got enough to share. Go out there into that world and find your own. You not getting none of this." She slid it back under her pillow, then laid her head back on the pillow and closed her eyes.

I wrapped my arms around myself. My body hurt. Tears ran down my cheeks. I felt so weak. My head was spinning. I needed that fix. I couldn't leave her room without getting it.

I stood up on weak legs and wiped my face. "Mama, give it to me. I'm not playing. I need it right now." I stepped closer to the bed, hugging myself. Snot slid out of my nostril. I could already feel the dope entering into my system. It would heal all of my pains, take away the agony of torture I was experiencing.

"I said what I said. Now, I'm not giving you a muthafucking thing. Get out of my room, son. Now!"

I couldn't do that. I was too sick. I had to have that heroin. My body needed it. I would pay her back. I'd buy her two ounces instead of one.

I got on the bed, straddled her, and slid my hand under the pillow, taking ahold of the heroin "I swear I'll pay you back, Mama. You know I'd never do this unless I really would." I made my way out of the bed.

She took ahold of my arm and dug her nails into my skin, scratching me until I bled. "Give me my shit, Jahrome. Don't do this to me. That's all I got left. I ain't got no husband. I ain't got no daughter. My leg is gone. Please, baby." She jumped on my back and bit into my neck. "Give me my shit!"

I flung her off and ran out of her room slamming the door behind me. "I'm sorry, Mama. I'll be back with a bunch more. I promise."

I rushed back into my room and found Yani sitting on the edge of the bed with her head down. I rushed into the bathroom and closed the door. I looked over the heroin, then realized I didn't have any works. "Fuck!" I hollered, feeling sicker. I rushed back into the room and got fully dressed with Yani trying to talk to me. I ignored her for as long as I could.

She grabbed me and I pushed her away. "Not right now, baby. I'll be right back. Don't be mad, I just gotta do something. Please chill."

I stepped back into the hallway just as my mother was sticking her head out of the door to see where I'd gone. She had tears in her eyes and was still naked.

"I can't believe you're going to do this to me, Jahrome. You don't care about me. All you care about is yourself."

I moved her out of the way. She fell to the floor, and I felt around her room until I found her works, then ran back out of there with her screaming at me that she hated me. That she had no son. The door slammed.

I ran down the stairs, and out to the parking lot. I jiggled the handle to Yani's truck, and thankfully it opened. Once inside, I got the dope ready, and two minutes later I was shooting it into my arm, with my eyes closed. The feeling of it entering my system was like I'd died and gone to heaven.

I remained in her truck for about thirty minutes, nodding out. Then I stepped out of it and went on the hunt for my poison that had me hooked. I felt good. My body was back working. The headache had gone. I was able to think as clearly as I possibly could. I had to find me and my mother some more.

I didn't feel like arguing with her when I got back. I already knew Yani was going to be all over my ass when I got back because I had just did her real bogus, and she wasn't the type to stand for that. Man, I needed to get ahold of myself.

It took me two hours before I was able to locate some halfway decent-looking young white boys who I figured were into the life. They were standing outside of a green van banging Metallica. They were three deep, and all of them had long hair and looked grungy.

I slid up on the one who was leaning against the

driver's door of the van. He nodded his head up and down and wore sunglasses even though it was a real cloudy day. I checked his arms for track marks and located a few. "Say, my guy, can I holla at you for a minute?" I asked, trying to sound as cool as I could.

He nodded. "Yeah, man, what's up?" He lowered the glasses on his young face. His eyes were beet-red. There were dark circles under them.

"Look, I'm not from around here, but I'm looking for a few ounces of some boy. You know where I can score that?"

He scrunched his face and looked me up and down, then looked over to his friends. They walked over to us and stood beside him. He looked me over again. "Hey, man, are you a cop or something?" He took his glasses off and slid them into his shirt pocket.

"What! Man, hell nall, I aunt no fucking cop. I'm a Blood! I don't fuck wit' police."

He laughed. "Well, excuse me, I've just never had a Colored come up to me looking to score some horse. I figured you were either a cop or just some stupid nigger looking to get his ass whooped."

He pushed me so hard I landed against the car that was parked on the side of his van. My back cracked an pain shot all over me.

"Get his money, man. This nigger wants to score a few ounces, so he must have a couple grand on him."

I straightened up and swung a right hook as hard a I could, connecting with his jaw and breaking it. I literally felt it shatter under my fist. He fell to his right and crumbled to the ground. I stomped him in the face, my Jordans further crushing his shit. "Bitch-ass kracker. You think it sw–"

Bam! "Nigger!"

One of the bigger white boys hit me so hard I was seeing stars. He'd hit me right on the side of my chin, rocking me like he was a savage. I fell to one knee, got up, and took off running, dizzy as hell. My vision was blurry. My legs felt like Jell-O.

I evaded them for two blocks, then took an alley. I was halfway down it when I realized the alley was closed off and nothing more than a dead end. As I made my way back out of it, three of the big white boys appeared with scowls on their faces. One-by-one they took off their shirts and cracked their knuckles.

I backed up and scanned the alley, looking for any form of a weapon I could find. My eyes landed on a two-by-four. I rushed over and picked that big boy up. "Come on, muthafuckas. Let's get it on. Y'all gon' have to kill me. I ain't going easy."

One of the big white boys with swastikas all over his body held up a hand toward his friends, warding them off. "I got this, boys. You know I love pain. Let's get it on, monkey man." He smashed his fist into his hand and walked over to me, looking as if he was in a zone. "Swing, bitch!"

He didn't have to tell me twice. I swung the two-by-four as hard as I could, cracking him on the side of the head with it. To my surprise, the board broke, and he started bleeding like crazy.

"You motherfucker!" He jumped up and rushed me with his head down, picking me up in the air and running with me until my back crashed into the brick wall that closed the alley off. It knocked the wind out of me.

He dropped me to the ground, and kicked me in the jaw. My face bounced off of the pavement. I heard a steady ringing in my ears, then he was picking me up over his head. "Argh!" He threw me against the wall again.

I was hurting all over. I slowly staggered to my feet with my guards up. Wasn't no way I was about to let this kracker whoop me. Yeah, I was fucked up, but going now and admitting a white boy had whooped my ass would sound worse than anything else. I wasn't going.

"Oh, so you want some more? Okay, come and get it, nigger boy." He skipped on his feet and threw a heavy haymaker, aiming for my head. I mean, it seemed like he was trying to take it off.

I ducked just in time. The force of his punch sent him twisting sideways. I used that to my advantage. With all the force I could muster, I punched him so hard in the temple with my right hand that his eyes got bucked, and he fell to his knees with his mouth open. Then he fell on his face, out cold.

I rushed over and stomped him on the back, then kicked him in the ribs. "Get yo' punk-ass up. This ain't over. Come on, white boy." *Bam!* I stomped him again. Then again. And again. His face danced off the sidewalk.

The other white boys ran over and held up their guards. Then, one-by-one, they rushed me, swinging like crazy. I was hit in the face. Then the jaw. Then I swung and connected with one of their jaws, and then another's face. Every time I would land a punch, I would receive two. It got so bad I got tired of swinging. I grew weak. I was also tired of getting hit over and over again, so I said 'fuck that.' I went berserk, swinging as fast and hard as I could, then took off running.

Blood ran out of my nose and I could taste it in my mouth, but I had to get out of there. A smart man knew when to retreat so he could live to see and fight another day. I was running so fast I was bumping into people and everything. I looked over my shoulder to see the white boys chasing me. My lungs were hurting.

I didn't know how much stamina I had left inside me. Finally, I did the pussy thing. I ran into a lot full of police and stopped, leaning over with my hands on my thighs, breathing heavily.

The white boys stopped at the entrance of the parking lot and looked over at me. Some of them had busted eyes or noses. Their hair was all screwed up, and their bodies were red. Just like I was fucked up, so were they, and it was more of them than it was of me. They looked heated.

I held up two middle fingers and took off jogging toward the hotel. I had plans of coming back and murdering every one of them. I would never forget what they did to me.

Chapter 10

"You're going to lose your mind, Heinous. I don't tell you what's good because you're going to lose it, I just know it," Yani shouted.

She was down on her knees in front of the bathroom door when I stepped out of the shower. I needed to wash the blood off of me. I had so many scrapes and bruises that the shower was painful every time the soap touched one of my wounds.

I tightened the bath towel around my body. "Baby, what are you talking about?" I asked. My head began to pound. I had yet to find us some more dope.

"Baby, can you promise me you're going to be strong, no matter what I tell you? Please. I need you strong for us right now." Her face was full of tears. She wiped them away.

Now I was getting a little worried. "Baby, chill. Tell me what's good before I freak the fuck out. I'm not playing. What's up?"

She slowly stood up and placed her hands in front of her as if she was praying to me. "Come here, and I need you to be strong. Know that I'm here for you, and I always will be until the bloody end. You're my everything, and I'll be by your side, always."

I swallowed and allowed her to guide my hand. She took the key card and slid it into the slot that connected to my mother's room. The light flashed green, but before she pushed the door in, she looked over her shoulder at me. "I got you, boo."

I was over all that build-up shit she was trying to

pull. I nudged her out of the way and pushed the door in to my mother's room. I was met by the strong stench of her unwashed room, which was completely darkened. Not even a candle burned.

"Mama! Mama, where you at?" I shouted, making my way through the room.

"Try the bathroom, Heinous. Please, don't freak out," Yani whimpered.

"Shut up, Yani! Damn! You fucking wit' my head more than this situation. Toughen yo' ass up!" I snapped and rushed past the expanse of the room and into the bathroom. I pushed the door open. As soon I did, my eyes traveled inside of the bathroom. "Mama, you in here?" I pushed the door open just a tad more and stepped inside.

I could hear Yani beside me, sobbing. I was seconds away from kicking her ass. Seriously. All that emotional shit was getting on my nerves, especially since I didn't know what she was getting so emotional about.

But then I stepped inside far enough and dropped to my knees in tears. "Aw, come on!"

There was my mother, lying naked in the bathroom tub with water inside of it. Both of her wrists were slit, as well as the side of her neck. Her eyes were closed. Her head was bent awkwardly to one side.

I broke all the way down for thirty minutes, crying my heart and eyes out. Then I got up and got in the tub with her. I wrapped her in my arms and rocked back and forth with my eyes closed. First it was my father, then my best friend, then my sister, and now my mother. I felt like the angel of death was really following me around.

I rocked my mother back and forth into the wee hours of the night. Yani sat beside me on the floor, rubbing my arm. She'd cried for a few hours, then rested her head on the rim of the tub and dozed off from exertion. I was thankful she was still alive. I needed her. I had to figure out a way to get our lives back on track. We were all we had left.

Instead of calling the police and ambulance over my mother, I decided to get rid of her body myself. Unfortunately, I had to dismember her limbs before burning them in a metal garbage can outside of Zion, Illinois. After I let them burn for a straight hour, I dug the big pieces of her out of the garbage can and dropped them into the Chicago River. Throughout the whole process I broke down and had to stop several times.

The reason I'd chosen to burn and dump her body was because, in my eyes, I was already on the run for multiple murders. I didn't need the police any further inside of me and Yani's business. I was already hanging onto my freedom by a piece of thread. I needed to be out so I could protect my queen, so we cleaned my mother's room from top to bottom before paying our bill and leaving.

We wound up in a Hilton hotel outside of Chicago. Yani sat on the edge of the hotel bed with her head lowered. "I don't know how much more I can take of this, Heinous." Her eyes were bucked, staring off into space.

I took my shirt off and dropped it on the chair inside of the room. Along the way I'd managed to pick up an ounce of China, and I couldn't wait to do my thing. My body was calling for it. "What's the matter with you, Yani? Why you sound so defeated?"

She covered her face with both of her hands and sighed loudly. "I'm tired. This ain't the life I wanted to live. I wanted to make something of myself, and I thought you did, too. I would have never imagined this would wind up being our life. Everybody dropping like flies all around. We're on the run for our lives, me miserable and you strung out on some fucking dope. I can't take any more of this." She lowered he head further, placing her face on her lap.

I came around and stood in front of her. My throat was dry. My body felt tingly. "Baby, I ain't strung out. What would make you think that?" I asked, feeling some type of way.

She lifted her head out of her lap. "Yes, you are, Heinous. Your mother told me what you did. You would have never done that unless that heroin had you by the throat, and I never thought I'd see the day. Seriously."

I watched her for a long time, fien'ing for my next fix. I didn't know what to say to her, but if I was high, I knew the words would form so perfectly. I couldn't think without my dope in my system. I just couldn't. "Baby, I just needed to get away whenever I feel like I was overwhelmed. I just got a whole lot going on. I'm under a lot of pressure. You can't begin to know what that feels like."

She stopped mid-pace and mugged me with hatred. "Are you fucking kidding me right now, Jahrome? Are you?"

I scratched my arm and exhaled loudly. "Here we go with this shit. Man, I don't feel like arguing with you right now, Yani. I just lost my mother. Where the fuck is your compassion?"

She scrunched her face and stormed toward me. "Nigga, yo' mama did that shit because of all of the shit you've taken her through. You pushed her over the edge by taking her dope from her right after she'd lost her daughter. I've been standing by your side since day one, negro. I knew you had a fucking problem, but I kept my mouth shut. I kept my mouth shut because I love you, and I was willing to overlook everything you've done because you are my man. You're in here, Heinous." She slapped her hand over her chest. "But you're fuckin' up, and I'm done. I can't take this shit no more."

I lowered my head. "So, I guess everybody's death is all on me, huh? Had it not been for Ol' Jahrome, they'd all still be alive and partying away, right, Yani?" I felt like I was about to break down. She was the last person I had left, and if I was about to lose her, it was over with for me.

"You know what I'm saying, Heinous. I ain't got time for you to fuck with my head so you can invoke some kind of sympathy from me. That's yo' problem. You ain't got nobody to tell you when you're doing wrong. Well, I am. I don't know if father's murder was really your fault, but I know that Leah, our mother, and Brat's was. You've admitted to hers yourself. I'd be a damn fool if I stuck around. I know I'm next in line. For some reason you can't die, but everybody else around you can," she scoffed and continued to pace. "Fucking up my life. I ain't dying."

Now I was getting irritated. I felt like she'd been

feeling this way all along and had been faking the love. "Why don't you shut your ass up? You're pissing me off right now."

She shrugged her shoulders. "I don't care, Heinous. Anytime somebody tell your ass the truth, you're quick to wanna hurt them. Well, I'm here. I'm standing beside you, and I'm telling you that you're fucking up big time. It's not okay. I'm 99% sure I'm about to leave your ass. I don't even care about the money. You can keep that shit," she mumbling to herself. "I can't spend a single penny of it if I'm dead. Fucking around with you, I will be. Matter fact let me pack my shit. I'm outta here." She opened the closet and took her suitcase out of it, tossing it on the bed.

Now I was really heated. "Yani, I'm letting you know right now, you ain't about to leave me. You're all I got left. Before I let you leave me, I'll kill yo' ass. I mean that shit."

"On the real, Jahrome, if I stay wit' yo' ass, I'ma wind up dying anyway. So you might as well get me out of the way. I ain't scared of you and nobody else. Nigga, do what the fuck you gotta do. That's on my mother." She opened the suitcase and threw all of my clothes out of it and onto the bed.

I growled, grabbed the suitcase, and threw it against the wall. "Bitch, you aunt going nowhere! You're all I got left. I ain't going. Fuck that!"

She avoided eye contact with me and looked at the floor with a blank stare. I could tell she was angry. Her chest heaved up and down. She clenched and unclenched her fists. Her eyes watered.

"So, what you gon' do, Jahrome? You gon'

strangle me? Shoot me? Or are you going to stab me to death? How are you going to take me out of my misery? Because I'm –"

"Look, Yani, I don't want to hurt you, period. I know I been fucking up, but I'ma get better. I swear I am. I just can't have you leaving me. I need you, man. Damn. Can't you see that shit?" My voice was breaking up. My throat was so tight I could barely talk. "I need you."

Her face was full of tears again. She lowered her head. "I don't know how much longer I can handle all of this. We're on the run. You're saying this detective is gon' lock you up for the rest of your life, and he has the evidence to do so. On top of that, every big wig in Chicago is looking to gun you down. You haven't said anything about escaping to another part of the country, or maybe even out of the country. And I know you're planning on going back into Chicago because we're literally less than thirty miles away from the city. It just seems like we're fighting a losing battle here. How many more people have to die before you see what's dead smack in front of your face?"

I didn't know what to say to her at that point. Everything she'd said made perfect sense. I didn't have any legs to stand on, so instead of arguing any further with her, I sat on the bed beside her and put my arm around her. "You're right, baby. Everything you've just said is right. I mean, I been fucking up big time. I should be in a better position, but instead I've only been a hindrance to us, so I'ma let you lead for a while. I'ma follow you because I trust you. Do you understand me?"

She turned and looked at me with excited eyes. "Don't sat that if you don't mean it, Heinous. You know how hard headed you are. If you've never listened to your parents, how the hell are you going to feel listening to me, your woman?"

I hopped up off the bed. "You don't know what I'm going through, the shit that goes through my head every second of every day. That's why you don't get me. But if you just knew a little of what I feel in here, then you'd understand. You don't fucking get it. But yeah, I see that I'm not right right now, so as long as you're going to remain my woman, I'd prefer to let you lead. At least until I can get my mind back, because right now I'm so gone that I don't even know who I am anymore."

She turned to me and knelt between my legs. "Baby, calm down. I'm not trying to make you feel like shit. I love you. I really, really do. I know you can lead the way, but it's like you said, your mind is all clogged up. But you're a warrior, Jahrome. I know you love me and you loved your family. Baby, I'm not downplaying your strength. We been through a whole, whole lot. It's not fair for me to judge your strength."

I needed to get my head right. I needed a fix. I kissed Yani on the forehead and stood up. "Let me know what you want us to do and where we're goin'. I won't put up a fight, I promise."

I left her sitting on the bed and went into the bathroom to get myself right, shootin' more of the heroin than I had in the past. By the time I came out of the bathroom, I was high as a kite. I mean super, super high. I was feeling good, and how! I'd shot so much dope that while shooting my last portion of it, I felt my heart beating so fast that I refused to push the feeder of the syringe all the way down, so I still had a nice amount in the syringe. I figured I'd save it for later.

I knew in order for me to be led by my woman, I was going to need to be high all the time. I was an alpha male. I was used to being the leader. I'd refused to follow any man for as long as I could remember, and I'd always had a problem with authority figures in life. But I loved Yani. She was my heart, and if all it took was me letting her lead for her to stay, then I was all for it.

When I came out of the bathroom, she was laying in the bed, asleep and snoring lightly. I imagined it had been a few long weeks for her. I climbed into the bed beside her and slid works into the bedside table drawer, praying she wouldn't' look inside and discover it. I saw the way she looked like she was disgusted when she talked about my habit. It made me feel some type of way. To have her look at me in disgust was like a gut punch. It knocked all of the wind out of me.

I felt so alone and like no one would ever understand the mental battles that went on in my head. Not only were the souls from the lives I'd taken over the years haunting me, but then there were those of my immediate family. When I closed my eyes, I saw one of their dead bodies or faces. It was getting so bad that I even hated to blink. My only oasis, my only escape, was the heroin. I needed it to function. It was the only thing that made sense.

Yani rolled onto her side, and flung her arm

across my waist. I rubbed it up and down as I listened to her snore just loud enough for me to hear. She sounded as if she was sleeping good from being exhausted for a long time.

I felt like I was all alone and trapped in darkness, falling and falling into an abyss with no bottom. Even though she slept in the bed beside me, there was no one in that room but me. The heroin had me locked down and stranded on an island of dependence and agony. I felt sick being the only one present on its land.

So I did the unthinkable without finding the way through. A tear dropped from my eye.

I opened the drawer on the side of me and pulled out the syringe that still had about an eight of liquid heroin inside. I popped the cap and took ahold of Yani's hand, placed the needle into the thickest vein on her hand, and pushed it in. As soon as I saw a hint of her blood, I pushed down the feeder and pumped the heroin into her system as my tears rolled off of my chin and onto the sheets. Then I yanked it out and placed it back into the drawer.

She jerked in her sleep, then yanked her hand away. Her eyes shot open. She grabbed her right, wounded hand. "What did you just do, Heinous? What did you just do?" She threw the covers back and hopped out of the bed with just her white beater on. I could see she was without any bra or panties. With every movement, her titties jiggled in her shirt. Both of her nipples poked through the beater, which was so short that all of her thick thighs were on display. Right above them was her bald, dark brown pussy.

I got up. "Baby, calm down. I just wanted you to try it. In order for you to lead me, you gotta be on the same wavelength." I wiped my nose. I was super high.

She staggered on her feet and held her arms. I began to feel loopy. There was this music in my head that had almost taming me like a Snake Charmer. My head was spinning.

"I can' believe you would did this to me, Jahrome. I can't." She backed up to the wall and slid down it, until her knees were up against her chest.

Hood Rich

Chapter 11

I could hear her crying behind her arms. Her brown lips were slightly displayed beneath her. "Why did you do this to me, Heinous?"

I crawled across the floor and stuck my head right between her opened thighs. Her position had that cat looking fat, like a nice, juicy, dark brown peach. I sniffed it. She smelled of kitty with a hint of perfume.

"Baby, I just wanted you to go there with me one time. How can you lead me if you don't know what's going on in my head? Just relax, boo. Enjoy the feeling so you can learn how to master it, then you can master me. I love you so much." I sucked her thick sex lips into my mouth with my head leaning to the side. My tongue traveled up and down in between her groove, tasting her saltiness. It excited me.

"Un! Stop! Get away from me. I'm so high, it tingles so much. Why? Why would you do me like this?" She held her knees and closed her eyes.

I opened her folds and sucked at her pink, darting my tongue in and out of that pussy. Her scent got heavier an heavier the more I reached with my tongue. My nose bumped her hard clitoris, wetting me. Her thick thighs shivered and spread wide. I slurped at her juices. "I'm sorry, boo. Daddy's sorry, but I had to get us on the same level. You'll be able to lead better now. I swear." I dug my face further into her pussy.

She beat at me with her fist. "Un! No! I'm not giving you none. You can't have it. Not right now. Stop."

I grabbed both of her thighs, pulled her right

back, and forced her knees to her chest. Now her pussy was really heavy in the air. With her knees to her breasts, it busted her gap wide open, so much so I could see pink between the brown labia lips. I laid my forehead right on her black hairs and flickered her clitoris, toying wit it. I knew while I was on the dope, the most sensitive part of me was the helmet of my piece. That was the equivalent to her clitoris, so I had plans on spending as much time on it as I had to. I needed to get Yani hooked all over again. I couldn't have her break bad on me. I needed her to understand, needed her to get where I was coming from. I didn't want to die alone and trapped all by myself any longer, as selfish as that may have seemed. I was just being honest.

I opened her lips as far as they could go and sucked on her clitoris as if it were a nipple. I nipped at it with my teeth, flicked my tongue back and forth over it. It tasted like she was peeing in my mouth. I got geeked and went on.

"Uh! Uh! Jahrome! Jahrome! Aw shit!" she screamed, threw her head back, and started to cum all over my face, squirting her juices into my mouth, and all over my cheek. "Stop, Daddy. Stop. I can't handle this right now. Please," she cried.

My tongue stabbed between her folds over and over. I sucked her clit into my mouth, popped it out, and flicked it some more, then rubbed my face all over her twat, loving the feel of it.

She bucked into me, sat up, and scratched me across the back before falling back on her elbows. "Uh! What you waiting on? Fuck me! Please! You got my pussy tingling!" She squeezed her breasts together and yanked the beater above them so she could play with her distended nipples. They protruded from her mounds at least an inch. She sucked one into her mouth and licked around her nipple.

I opened her ass and licked around her anus, slid my finger inside of it, then followed that with my tongue. Her juices leaked out of her box and onto the carpet. Then I was sucking all over her stomach, darting my tongue into her belly button, working my way back down south.

Forcibly, I turned her onto her stomach and opened that fat ass wide, displaying her rose bud. I placed my lips right over it and sucked hard, my tongue darting into her and sawing it in and out.

Her hand reached under her stomach and between her legs, tweaking her clitoris. Pulling on it. "Daddy, please fuck me. Fuck your baby now. I can't take what you're doing to me. I can't handle it. I need you."

I pushed her hand out of the way, and held her ass cheeks, which felt hot in my hands. She was spread. She looked nice and thick. Her juices were pouring out of her richer than I'd ever saw them before. It looked so good to me. Her scent got heavier as well. I took my nose and stuck it in her pussy hole and inhaled as hard as I could. Then I was sucking on her jewel like a juicy oyster, praying to taste her cum again. I was fien'ing for it. Needed it.

"Cum for Daddy, Baby girl. Cum for me. Please, boo." I attacked that clit with every technique I could think of. I trapped it between the gap in my teeth and played with it, swallowing her juices along the way.

Yani rose to her knees, shaking like crazy. "I'm 'bout to cum. I told you to leave me alone!" she wailed and busted all in my face, beating her fist on the floor while I sucked at her jewel until she fainted on her stomach.

I licked down her thick thighs and laid the side of my face on the floor, sucking her toes into my mouth one at a time. "Baby, I'm sorry. You hear me? I'm sorry. I just wanted you to feel me on a higher level."

I got up and picked her up, tossed her on the bed, and got between her legs. My dick was throbbing. I got buck naked and rubbed the big head up and down in between her crease. Her cat was so wet that more than once my head nearly slipped into her entrance.

She closed her eyes and winced in sexual readiness. "Please give it to me. I'll forgive you as long as you give it to me. Please. I need it so fucking bad. Your baby needs you."

I leaned down with my dick rubbing against her mound. It jumped. I sucked on her neck and dragged my teeth across it. "You forgive your daddy, baby? Tell me the truth." I slipped the head in a little bit, then pulled it back out.

She popped her thighs open as far as they could go. Her hand wandered down between her legs and tried to slip her fingers into her hole, but I moved her hand out of the way. "Daddy! Please, I need you. I need you so bad." She humped into the air and groaned. "I can't take this shit. Fuck me or kill me. Now!"

I placed the head on her entrance again. It slipped into her hole. Her lips were open like a wet rose. Clear gel leaked out of them and ran over her rose bud below before dripping off her lower back onto the sheets.

I pulled my dick back out. "Baby, tell me you forgive me. That you understand. You know I never meant to hurt you. You're my baby. Nothing matters more than you, Yani. Please. I need to hear those words."

She slid her hands around my waist and dug her nail into my sides so deep I knew I would be bleeding when she pulled them out. "I understand. I swear I do. Now, please have sex with your baby. Please put it in my li'l hole. Stretch me open. Please!" She screamed and drug her nails across my skin.

I felt the blood dripping own me. I picked up my pipe and cocked backward so I could see her cat. The big head nestled between her lips. She wrapped her hand around the stalk at the same time I drove my hips home, burying myself deep into her womb, her warmth searing me like a velvet fireplace.

"Shit!" She came shaking and squeezing her big titties together.

The nipples were even longer now. I had to suck them while I fucked, had to appreciate this body for all it was worth, and in my mind it was worth so, so much. I got to ramming her kitty, holding onto the top of the headboard for leverage, cheating and not caring. I dug as deep as my pipe could go.

She sat up and licked my chest, fell backward again, and screamed, cumming all over me. Her pussy walls tightened around my pole like a greasy fist, pumping and pulling. Her breasts wobbled up and down on her chest.

Every time I slid forward, she humped upward to

get the best I could offer her. Her scent, the sight of her perfect, sexy-ass body, a d the feel became too much for me. I pushed her knees to her chest and got to hammering away as fast as I could, feeling closer to the ultimate euphoria.

There was a loud squelching. Her kitty queefed, and I kept on slamming. "Baby! Here Daddy cum. Here Daddy cum, Momma. Ah, shit!" I growled and started to shake as my seed flew out of me and into her over and over in thick globs. It felt so good. My stomach locked up and then released. I stayed planted deep within her womb.

About three minutes later, I pulled out. Yani stayed on her back with her thighs wide open. rubbing her pussy. Then she stuck her thumb into her mouth, an turned on her side away from me. That alarmed me. I wondered if she was starting to hate me for what I had done to her. Even I was having regrets. I was wishing I'd never shot the heroin into her system.

I crawled over her body, and tried to turn her so I could see her face. "Baby, what's the matter? Are you mad at me now?" I asked, feeling sick and irritated because my dick was still rock hard.

"I just don't know why you would do me like that, Jahrome. I thought I was your baby. One of us has to have a clear head. Now that this stuff is in my system, we're both goin to be screwed up mentally. We're destined to fail. I'm sorry now." She took the pillow and pulled it over her heed.

I took the pillow and threw it across the room. "Yani, I said I was sorry. I didn't mean it, baby. What do you want me to do? I'll do whatever as long as you forgive me."

"It's too late now, Heinous. I mean it, it's too late now. It's already in my system. I don't know what we can do besides deal with it. I'm just shocked you would do me like this." She rolled onto her back and looked up at me with red eyes and tears flowing down her cheeks. "I'll be okay, though."

I shook my head and exhaled, looking into her eyes. "Baby, I swear I'm sorry. I just needed you to understand me mentally, that's all. Now you'll know how to lead me."

She shook her head. "No, I don't want to lead you. I don't know how to lead a man anywhere. My father sucked. Just don't get us killed, Daddy. I won't leave you. I swear I won't live without you. You're all that I know or would want to know. You're my life. We've been through so much together." She sat up and pulled me down, wrapping her legs around my body. "Daddy, can you make slow, passionate love to me? No fucking because I'm hurting. I just need you to take me away from here. Allow me to lose myself within you. Please. I am drowning." She opened her thighs to me.

I kissed her soft lips, then licked them. I sucked them into my mouth as my piece went slowly in and out of her as if I was churning butter. "I. Love. You. Boo. Daddy. Love. You. So. Much. And. I'm. Sorry. I'm. So. So. Sorry," I stroked.

She cried underneath me nodding her head. "Un. Un. I know. I know, Heinous" was all she said throughout our entire lovemaking session.

After two more hours of sex, we both passed out, breathing heavy against one another.

Hood Rich

***

"Heinous, Wake up. Please wake up," were the first words I heard the next morning. I opened my eyes to see Yani standing over me with her hair wild on her head. She scratched her arm and shivered.

"Baby, what's good?" I asked, sitting up on my elbows with my eyes squinting from the sun that was shining in through window in the room. It had my head pounding within seconds. I put my hand up to block its rays or I was about to throw up.

She bit her fingernail and looked down on me nervously. "I. Do it to me again. Please," she asked.

Just the thought of having sex so soon made my dick hurt. I wasn't wit' it. Yeah, Yani was fine as a muthafucka and I could hit that pussy all day long and never get tired, but my piece felt like it was raw. I didn't care is she didn't give me no more pussy for a week. I would be good.

I shook my head. "Baby, yo' pussy the bomb, but I ain't ready. My shit hurt. You gotta let me regroup, damn. Get some sleep." I turned on my side and closed my eyes. "And shut that fucking blind. That sun gon' make me throw up." I already felt my stomach turning over and over. I felt like I needed to shit, too.

She fumbled with the blinds, and then the room was dark. Behind my eyelids it was no longer red from the sun shining against them. Now there was nothing but blackness, just like I liked it to be.

I felt a presence looming over me, and then she was shaking my shoulder. "Please! I'm not talking about sex. I'm talking about the boy. I need some more of it in my system. I need to feel like I felt last night. Take me away from here again. Now I see why you do it." She got down on her knees. "Either you give me some more, or I'ma go and find it myself. I don't want to do that."

"Yani, you better stop playing with me. If you take yo' ass out of this hotel tonight, I'ma track you down and fuck you up. I mean that shit. Now try me," I warned.

"Then get yo' ass out of that bed and give me some more. You the one who got me hooked on this shit. I didn't know nothing about it until last night. Now I need some more of it!" she snapped and pulled the covers off of me, exposing my nudity. She jumped on the bed and straddled me, hugging me. "Please. It felt so good. I wanna go there again."

My eyes were opened wide. What the fuck had I done? I had never seen her act like that before. She was scaring me. "Awright, baby girl, just let me go and I'll get you squared away." I wiggled from under her and stood up, looking over t her. She was on her knees in the bed, naked, a frightened look on her face.

She bit on her fingernail. "I love you, baby."

"I love you too, Boo."

It took me five minutes to get her syringe filled with the poison. She sat with her back up against my chest while we sat against the headboard. I fed the needle into a thick vein in her forearm before I injected the heroin into her system.

She moaned louder the more I pushed down on the plunger. "Thank you, baby."

Hood Rich

Then she fell back against me, smacking her lips.

Chapter 12

The following day, I was awakened by a knocking on the hotel door. I threw on the terry cloth robe that the hotel issued to all patrons, then made my way to the door. "Who is it, Jo?" I rubbed the sleep out of my eyes and yawned into my fist. My breath didn't smell so good, either. I peeped that right away. That wasn't okay.

"It's me, Jahrome. Detective Taylor. Don't try and do anything stupid. I know you're in there with Yaniece, so just open the door so we can get an understanding."

I looked into the peephole and saw the detective standing in the hallway in front of the door with an irritated look on his face. I tried to scan the rest of the hallway, but the little hole wouldn't allow for me to do so. I started itching right away. "Awright man, but let me get my bitch dressed. Hold fast, nigga."

I rushed to the bed and tapped Yani's thigh. "Baby. Baby. Wake up. Wake up right now. I need you to get dressed."

She waved me off. "Not right now, Baddy. I can't think straight." She put her forearm over her eyes and snored lightly again. Her legs opened wide, exposing her sex lips.

I smacked her thigh just as Taylor started to beat on the door. "Baby, get up. That detective I was telling you about is here. Now if he snatch me up and you wake up not knowing what the fuck took place, you gone freak out. So get yo ass up!" I pulled her wrist and made her sit up.

She started crying. "I'm so sleepy. Baby, all I

wanna do is sleep. I ain't never been this tired before." She said this without opening her eyes. "Why is he here?" she asked, her eyes closed. Then her head dropped and she was snoring slightly

I pushed her ass back with a huff. Her head landed on the pillow, and she didn't pick it back up.

I strode over to the door and yanked it open. "What the fuck you looking so stupid for? And how did you find me?" I asked, moving out of the way for him to enter the room. He walked past me, and I could smell his manly-ass cologne. It made me gag. I hated the smell of men.

He stopped mid-stride and pinched his nose. "Damn! Y'all need to open a window in this place. It reeks!" he shouted, looking down on me in disgust.

"Yeah, well, that's what good fucking smell like. Now, answer my question? How did you find me?" I wanted to know.

He strolled further into the room and looked across the expanse of it, eyeing the sleeping Yani. She'd been moving so much that the covers had moved down, exposing her supple breasts. I could see the definition of her thick nipples from the doorway, so I could only imagine what he was able to make out.

"Mm, that's one fine li'l sista in there. They don't make 'em like that no more." He stopped to enjoy the view, and even though I couldn't blame him because she was that damn bad, it got me irritated and ready to smoke his pig-ass.

I locked the door and rushed into the bedroom section of the room. I threw a blanket over her that covered her all the way to her forehead. Due to our circumstances I was falling more and more in love with her. I didn't want this dude's bitch-ass, or any nigga for that matter, lusting after her. She belonged to me. That was that.

Taylor laughed and took a seat on the love seat. "Been tracking you ever since you and those white boys go into a fight back in Waukegan. You think I trust you enough to not track your every fucking move?" he asked pulling out a cigarette.

I sat on the bed. "Why are you here?" I was defeated.

He lit the cigarette and blew the smoke toward the ceiling. "Well, first of all, you're coming with me back to Chicago. Now. Secondly, when you get there, you're going to kill Pesos. After you complete the task of murdering him, you'll bring me all of the money you are set to recover on this endeavor, and depending on how I feel around that time, I'll elect to give you a certain percentage that will make me happy. How does that sound?" He looked past my shoulder and frowned. "That's nice. What I wouldn't do for a piece of that."

I looked behind me to see Yani had kicked the covers completely off of her body. Her thighs were spread, her pussy on full display. Her hand rested slightly to the right of it. Her scent wafted into the air.

I covered her back up and mugged him. "Say, Blood, you can keep them predator-ass comments to yourself. Take yo' big, black ass home to your wife, nigga." I was fuming, my heart beating heavy in my chest, making it hard for me to breathe and calm down.

Taylor laughed. "If I wanted your little girlfriend, I'd simply lock you up and throw away the key. Then I'd promise her the world just to get in between them thighs. After I cum, I'd lock her ass up, too, for being an accessory to everything you've done that she knows about. That's how I get down. It won't be the first, nor the last time." He sat back in the sofa.

I eyed him with building hatred. I wondered what he looked like with multiple slugs in his face. Or maybe with his eyes plucked out and thrown on the floor in front of him. I wanted to torture this punk, fuck him over in a major way. Maybe shove a shotgun up his ass and pull the trigger. That would be cool.

"I'ma give you a half an hour to get your shit in order, then you're rolling out with me. Pesos has to be murdered before tomorrow afternoon. If he's allowed to meet with the head of the Mala Noche Cartel, Chicago will be destroyed. I can't allow for that to happen, so you gotta put this fire out. It's that simple. Now, g'on 'head and holler at your girl. The clock is ticking." He smiled and rose from the sofa. "Unless you want me to wake her up? I ain't got no problem wit' that." He laughed and made his way toward the bed, looking predatory.

Yeah, I was gon' kill this bitch-ass nigga. He wanted to be playing with my baby? We was gon' see about that. I blocked his path and mugged him with hatred.

"Bitch-ass pig, if you lay a finger on my woman, I'ma torture you before I kill you in cold blood. You been following me long enough to know I ain't the one to be played with. Meet me by the door."

He rested his hand on his service weapon and looked into my eyes as if he was about that life. I didn't know if he was or not, but if he touched Yani, I was about to find out. I was gon' be all over his ass with nothing but murder on my mind. I could taste the kill of him already.

"Like I said, Jahrome, you got thirty minutes." He stepped out of my face and into the hallway.

***

It took me twenty minutes to get Yani up enough so she could understand what was about to take place. As soon as it clicked, she broke into a fit of tears. "Hell nall. Why do you have to go with him back to Chicago? That man is leading you to your death. It's all kinds of money on your head. What if he's just turning you in for the cash? Have you thought of that?" She paced the carpet, her face red with anger.

I was already fully dressed with a bag of guns, money, and dope. I didn't give a fuck that I was rolling with a detective. He knew how I got down. If he had a problem with it, then maybe I would use one of my pistols early and blow his shit back.

"Baby, I get why you're concerned, but there is no way around this. If I don't handle this bidness for him, then he's going to book me on all of those murders. Then I'll really be fucked in the game. At least this way I control my own destiny. If anything looks fishy, I know how to conduct myself and my tools to come from under that situation. I ain't new to this shit. I'd rather die than be sitting in a fuckin' cell for the rest of my life. You know that." I snatched her ass up and wrapped my arms around her small frame, holding her as tight as I could. "I love you, Boo. I'll be back."

"I'm just supposed to wait around for you like some child? No, I'm not." She wiggled out of my embrace and pushed me off of her. "Fuck that. You don't know that for sure. I gotta move on with my life because you're not coming back. I know you're not!" She mugged me, her head tilted to the side. "The fire escape, baby. Can't we just go down the fire escape?" She started to get dressed with her eyes bucked.

I grabbed her arms and held her out in front of me. "Baby, listen to me. I need you to have faith in me. Please. I'm not gon' let no nigga kill me. I'm a muthafucking animal, you know that. They done put slug after slug in me, and I'm still standing. I will be back, and we will emerge victorious. All I'm asking is that when I do, you be right here in this room, waiting on me. Then you can lead us for the rest of our lives. I'll follow you, boo. We can go and become whatever you decide. You have my word on that. All I care about is my baby girl, it'll be all about you from here on out." I rubbed the side of her face. "How about it? Do you trust me?"

"I'm so tired. I'm so, so tired." She lowered her head. "Heinous, I'm getting weaker, baby. All I want is to be happy. That's it, That's all. I don't know how much longer I can stand by your side like this. I mean, I love you. But." She exhaled loudly.

I held her face with both of my big hands. "Baby, just ride with me through this last storm. I promise after this there will be no more. If I'm lying, you can leave me, and I won't even chase you. Come now. Please." I got down on one knee, looking up at her and pleading.

She shook her head and rolled her eyes. "Damn you. How long will you be gone, Jahrome? I don't want to be stuck in this room waiting on you forever." She wiped away another lone tear.

"Only for a few days, boo. Today is Thursday. Give me until Monday. I should be back by then. Can you do that?"

She shook her head. "I guess I really don't have a choice now, do I?" She rolled her eyes again. I could see the little high school girl coming out of her. That same high school girl I had fallen in love with years prior. It was sexy to me.

"Nall, you don't." I smiled, feeling a small sense of relief.

She got down on her knees in front of me. "Jahrome, before you go, can you show me how to hook all that stuff up so I can at least stay high while you're not here? Its the only way I'm going to be able to do this whole waiting around thing. My anxiety is going to get the best of me. I just know it."

I looked into her eyes and got worried. Damn, I'd officially turned my woman out. I could see the anticipation in her eyes. The drug had a strong hold on her already. I worried that if I left her alone to shoot up on her own, she would overdo it and wind up either killing or hurting herself. But I knew I had to show her, because if I didn't, then I risked the chance of her trying to figure it out and pushing an air bubble into her veins. That was something I couldn't risk, either. I was in a no-win situation all because I had turned my woman into a using loser like me. Maybe when we got to the next place we'd enter rehab together and kick this nasty habit. I was definitely down for that.

"Alright, baby, but you have to pay close attention because if you make one wrong move, you could fuck around and kill yourself. Do you get that?"

She jerked her head back with her eyes bucked. "Fo' real? Like, as in dead-dead?"

I nodded. "Yeah, this stuff ain't nothing to play with, so watch me carefully." I spent the next ten minutes going over the process of shooting the heroin again and again until I was sure she had it down pat. Then I gave her an ounce of China White. "Baby, do not shoot more than this much of this shit an hour. Look." I placed about a quarter gram on the night table. "This is all you're going to need. Any more than that and you can overdose. Remember what happened to my mother before when she almost died?" I asked, rolling the ounce of heron up and putting it under her pillow.

She nodded. "Yeah, I remember. I'll be careful. I promise. All I'ma do is take a little and then go back to sleep. I'ma try to sleep until you get back here because being away from you is causing me to worry, and you're still right in front of me. Baby, please try and get back as soon as you can. Don't be lollygagging and fucking off with none of them project thots. You're down there to ice him and come home. You got it?" she asked, sounding like me.

I opened my arms wide and allowed her to sink

into them. "Yeah, boo, I got it."

I held her that way for a few minutes. My throat got tight, and I felt like breaking down. I didn't know what the future held for me in Chicago. All I knew was I had to survive so I could get back to my woman so we could start a new life where the murder and chaos could all be behind us. I wanted to do better and be better for her. I didn't know how we were going to kick our habits, but it was important we did.

"Baby, stay in the Apple store. Listen to as much music as you can and hit my phone whenever you're feelin' lonely. If I can, I'ma pick it up. And don't worry. I'ma be missin' you, too. I love you so fucking much, girl." I hugged her small frame into mine, her hot skin warming my cheek.

"I love you, too, Daddy, and I'll be right here when you get back. Just don't take forever."

"I swear as soon as I handle this bidness, I'll come running back to you. You're my everything." I tongued her down and made her go and get in the shower before I left.

Hood Rich

Chapter 13

I barely spoke a word to Taylor on our way back to Chicago. Yani was on my mind like crazy. I was sick over missing her already, which was odd because I had never been like that over a woman. I knew I would do anything for her, and I was silently praying it all went well. That I would be able to kill Pesos and get the hell out of the Windy City and back to her.

About fifteen minutes before we entered Chicago, Taylor turned to me with a smirk on his ugly-ass face. "I need us to get this thang over with, then you can go on with yo' life and I can go on with mine. We'll let bygones be bygones just as long as you stay out of Chicago. Now, that isn't too much to ask of you, is it?" He sat back in his seat, and turned on some old school Marvin Gaye. He started to nod his head like he had flavor or something. It irritated me.

"Nigga, for all I know you could be setting me up or dropping me right into the hands of my enemies. I know how you pigs get down. I don't trust none of you bitches. Never will. I don't care how much my back is against the wall." I laid my arm on the sill of my window

"You're worth more to me alive than dead, Jahrome. I need Pesos out of the game. It would be stupid of me to drop you off to them. Then what would I gain. Besides the three million dollars that's on your head, I guess." He snickered. "Nall, I need more than that. You'll see what I mean."

My phone buzzed. Yani had sent me a text saying she missed me already and I needed to hurry up.

She'd just taken a bit of medicine and was going to sleep. I sent her quick text back letting her know I loved her was going to do all I could to get back to her as soon as possible, then put my phone away.

I saw the El on its tracks in the middle of the highway. *I've come home,* I thought, shaking my head slightly.

"You was texting that dame back at the hotel, huh? I don't see why you wouldn't be. Damn. I don't think I could have torn away from her sexy ass. I'll tell you what, yo got more up willpower than I do. Have something that gorgeous I'd be in the bed all day and night long making sweet love. Yeah, that's what I'd be doing." He smiled.

I laughed to myself and nodded my head. "Is that right?" My heart was beating so fast I was struggling to breathe.

He smiled. "Yeah, that's right. But you ain't me. You're smarter than I would have been if I was in these streets, I'll give you that." He got into the fast lane and picked up speed.

I was seconds away from blowing his shit out. It took everything in me to not press my Glock to his temple and pull he trigger twice just to make sure I knocked his shit out. You wasn't supposed to fuck with or talk about a pure killer's woman. "For the last time, Taylor, keep my woman out of your mouth." This punk didn't know who he was fucking with. "This the only way all of this shit is going to work out. Awright? Follow that order or it's gon' be on. I'm not threatening you, either. I'm spitting big facts."

He held his hands shoulder-high. "Whew, awright, li'l brother. Well, at least I know you care about one life. I couldn't tell if you had a shred of decency in you, the way you sliced your mother up and burned her body into ashes." He curled his lip and kept on driving.

A chill went down my spine. I couldn't stop looking at him. How the fuck could he have known that? I made sure I was extra careful.

Instead of feeding into his bullshit, I side-stepped it like I'd done so many of his revelations before. "So, what is the game plan. Where are you taking me right now?"

I needed to get a grasp of what he had in mind. That way I could see what he was planning and alter it so I could make my own planning and execution. If there was one thing I'd learned growing up in Chicago, it was that a nigga always had to have his own plan of action. But the more I was able to get my opposition to expose their hand, the better my chances of survival. I'd murdered a nice amount of deadly foes because of their love of social media. They liked to run their mouths and brag about everything, exposing their hand and, nine time out of ten, their locations for this or that. It wasn't hard to hit a nigga up if I knew where he was going to be and what his intentions were when he got there. A comfortable enemy was the best kind for me. I loved whacking cats in their own habitat.

"Well, I'm dropping you off at an apartment complex on 113th and Prairie, right across the railroad tracks. You'll stay there until I give you a call. Pesos is set to have a meeting with Roman Velez tomorrow at ten in the morning. I'm going to leave it up to you to catch him either before or after he meets up with the prince of the Malo Noche Cartel."

He got off of the freeway at Cottage Grove and took 95th all the way down to Prairie before pulling up in front of the white apartment building I was to stay in. "So, what's it going to be?"

I looked around outside, paranoid. It was dark and there were no street lights on the block, but I knew for a fact I was in a Four Corner Hustler neighborhood. They're a deadly group of killers who ran under the five-point star. Their colors were gold and black, and their crew was about that life. Me and Brat had killed two of them last summer.

"Man, why the fuck you got me in this Fo' Hood? You already know us Bloods don't jam wit' these niggas. I thought you said you wasn't trying to get me killed?" I snapped, looking all around. I could barely see that far down the block, but I knew for a fact I was in the heart of their hood. Didn't no Blood nigga fuck with Prairie. We knew what it was.

Taylor snickered like a bitch. "Well, so far they the only mob in the city that ain't picked up the contract for your head. I don't know why they haven't, but they haven't. To me, that means this is the safest place for you. You're not going to be here long, anyway. This is one of our witness protection homes. It's under surveillance. If anything goes awry, we'll be here in less than a minute."

He looked down the street and flashed his high beams on and then off. The lights illuminated the street all the way down until I was able to see two police cars parked about ten houses down the road. That gave me bit of reassurance. I didn't think niggas would get stupid with the law right on the block. But then again, I'd murdered a nigga with the police on the corner before. Caught him slipping in his gangway and put two in the back of his head before jogging down the alley out of the way. No one could put shit past a Chicago nigga, that was a fact.

"A'ight, whatever, man. Which house am I going into? What time will you be hitting me up? I choose to murder him before he have that meeting, that way I can bounce this city before all of the vultures wake up."

"I got tabs on his monkey-ass, so let me get myself together and I'll be in touch with you sometime tonight, for sure. In the meantime, stay low and be ready to move at any time. You're going right there. The back door is unlocked." He pointed at a white house with a fence around it."

I grabbed my bag and stepped out of his car. "A'ight, catch you in a minute, then." I slammed the door as he pulled away from the curb. I ain't gon' even lie and say I wasn't spooked because I was. I had so much bad karma waiting on me in this city. I had murdered so many people and did so much shit that I felt like it was inevitable for me to reap what I'd sown. I just wasn't ready to reap yet. I was just figurin' out how much I really loved Yani. I wanted to explore that further. It felt so good to me to finally be able to care about somebody else besides myself or my family. She'd been there all along, and it took me almost losing all of them before I was able to see what I really had. That was messed up, but nothing short of the truth. I'd been immature this long, but felt like I was starting to get it.

I jogged up to the gate and hopped over it in one

movement, then ran along the side of the house. Somewhere across the street I could hear somebody bumping their gums, laughing as if they were at a comedy club.

I approached the door at the back of the house, then tried the knob, swinging it open. I took my Glock out of the bag and pushed in. Anybody who thought they could leave a door open in Chicago without somebody running in their crib was out of their mind. I had yet to see that not happen. I didn't give a fuck if this was a safe house or not. I wasn't about to take any chances.

I grabbed a flashlight out of my bag and held it up under my gun, slowly making my way up the stairs of the house, locking the door behind me. I was hoping there wasn't a cop or anybody inside, because I was ready to shoot and ask questions later, if even then.

I made my way up the first set of stairs and entered the main level of the house. It smelled like Febreeze. The floors were tiled and appeared clean. I saw a light switch right in the hallway that led to the kitchen. Instead of flipping it on, I walked right past it. Lights only meant I would expose myself. I wished I would have been lurking, waiting to kill a nigga in his crib and he was dumb enough to turn lights on, showing exactly where he was and wasn't. That would have been a plus for me.

I made my way all around that house in the dark until I was able to ensure I was the only person there. Once that was confirmed, I breathed a sigh of relief, took my ass into the living room, and plopped down on the couch. I pulled out my works and did a li'l dope. Not enough to fuck me up, just to put me in my murderous zone.

After I finished, I send a text to Yani asking if she was up or not. I waiting about five minutes, and then my phone was ringing. I saw it was her number, so I answered it. "Baby, hit me up on Snapchat so I can see you."

"I'm missing you like crazy."

She appeared on my phone minutes later. She looked happy and sleepy at the same time. "I miss you, li'l momma. How you holding up? Be honest with me." I scratched my arm and nodded out. That China White was so strong, though.

"I miss you every day. You already know that." She ran her fingers through her hair and sucked her bottom lip. "How are you holding up?"

"Well, I just got here a few minutes ago and had to make sure everything was good, but so far I'm Gucci. I'ma handle this bidness and hopefully be back that way in the morning. You already know I'm trying to get back to you as soon as possible. I miss you already, girl."

"I used a li'l bit more of that stuff. It got me super drowsy. I got in the tub, too, and damn near drowned. Just hurry up down there and get back to me. Can you do that?"

I nodded. "Gon', get you some sleep, boo. I'ma hit you up in the morning. Keep that door locked. Later."

"I love you, too, Daddy. Talk to you later."

Our Snapchat ended. As soon as it did, my phone rang right away. I looked at the face and saw Tanya's number come across the screen.

I picked it up right away. "What's good shorty?"
I stood up and began to pace back and forth with the
phone to my ear.

"This you, right, Heinous? You know who this
is?" she asked, speaking barely above a whisper.

"Yeah to both. I wouldn't be answering my
phone if I didn't know who you were. What's good?
You got somethin' for me."

She cleared her throat. "Yeah, I do, Lost Boy
here, and he tipsy as hell. I was thinking you could
handle this nigga tonight. I'm so tired of him
whooping my ass. I don't know what else to do," she
said with her voice cracking up.

"So, what you saying? I need you to holler at me
direct. That's how this shit work." I peeked out of the
curtains and watched a group of niggas about fifteen
deep walk past.

"You remember what we talked about? Well,
now is the best time. He got two suitcases over here,
and I think they're filled with more than money, too.
He supposed to make some kind of drop tomorrow.
I'm telling you, you should handle that biz tonight."

I waited until the group passed before I closed the
curtain all the way and sunk to the floor. "He at your
crib or his?"

"Mine, the same place School Boy stayed. But I
ain't seen him in a minute. I don't know where he
at." She paused for that to sink in, and it did. We were
on the same page.

I got to thinking over everything in my head. If I
killed Lost Boy's punk-ass and Pesos' within the
same twenty-four hours, I honestly felt a great
number of my beefs would be squashed. These were

my mortal enemies, niggas I knew thought about murdering me every single second of the day just like I thought about murdering them.

My head started to hurt. I didn't know what to do. Taylor had also told me to sit tight.

"How long that nigga been sleeping, and what he been drinking?"

"He on lean right now, and he been tooting all night before he got here. He fucked up. Been staggering around this house since he walked through the doors. Slapped me for no reason. I'm tired of this. Please do what you gotta do." She sounded like she was on the verge of tears, if not crying already. "Are you coming?"

Hood Rich

Chapter 14

It was two hours later when Tanya opened the door for me. A slight chill went down my spine, causing me to shiver. I could feel School Boy's soul roaming around this pad. The feeling was almost undeniable. She stuck her head out of the door, looking both ways. "Boy, I didn't even think you were coming. You had me worried. Come on in. He's upstairs on the couch, laid out like a fucking alcoholic."

Before I stepped inside, I peered over my shoulder at the blue Buick I had stolen, parked in the alley behind their house. I was making sure I had a clear path to get to it if anything was to go awry with murdering Lost Boy.

I was on high alert, ready for anything to happen. I took the Glock .40 out of my waistband, cocking it back, and pulling down the black ski mask I had bought for Pesos' murder. I stepped into the dark hallway of Tanya's crib, closing the door behind me.

She waved me to follow her. She was dressed in a robe that stopped just below her ample ass. There was a bulge in the front of it that made her look sexy to me.

She put a finger to her lips and pushed open the door to the house. She pointed. "He laying right in there on the couch. Can you see from here?" She took a step to her left and continued to point.

I followed her finger and stepped very close beside her, on high alert. The house was dark with the exception of a lamp shining in the living room where I guessed he was sleeping. It illuminated the couch. I could see a figure sprawled out on it, but his big arm was covering his face. I looked like dark skin, but I couldn't really make out who it was. That got me nervous.

I pulled Tanya to me and put the gun to her head, pressing it hard into her temple. She yelped and pissed on herself. I had my hand covering her mouth.

"Bitch, who the fuck is that in there? You sure that's Lost Boy?" I asked, growling into her ear. I didn't want to waste her, but if I had to do that in order to get out with my life, then that was going to happen. It was all about self preservation.

I moved my hand just enough to hear her speak. "It's him. He's asleep. Don't kill me, Heinous. You saved my life," she whimpered against me.

Many niggas who had been killed in the city had been set up by their own bitches or side chicks. It was the way the game worked, so it wasn't that I was doubting her or thought she wouldn't do it. I was also factoring in the amount of money that was on my head. There were very few people who wouldn't accept that bounty, so I tightened my hold on her and pushed her ass into the room. She led the way.

"Bitch, I swear to God if this ain't that nigga, I'ma kill his ass and take you off of this earth. Play wit' me if you want to."

I continued to walk forward toward the living room. The figure on the couch got closer and closer until I was only a few feet away from him. Now that I was able to see him more clearly, I confirmed it was Lost Boy. His arm covered his head, and he smelled horrible, almost as if he shit on himself. I gagged, then looked closer nearly losing my hold on her neck.

That's when I saw the blood stain. I was trying to

make some sense of it. How the fuck could he be bleeding already? I shook my head to think, and then I felt a presence looming behind me.

Out of instinct, I turned and held Tanya in front of me. Before I could even see who it was, I started bustin' in his direction. *Boom. Boom. Boom.* Then my eyes focused like a penned-in predator.

He was tall, in all black with a hood around his face. Two guns, one in each hand.

Boom. Boom.

The next two bullets from my gun slammed into his chest and opened it, throwing him back against the wall where he fell with his eyes wide open, dropping the guns.

That punk bitch had tried to set me up. I should have known hos were the worst. "Bitch, who else is here? Tell me. Who else is here?" I asked, jerking her around, then dragging her through the house, kicking in the two bedroom doors and finding the rooms empty upon inspection.

I wound up back in the living room, choking Tanya's ass out. I squeezed harder and harder, pulling upward while she fought and kicked her legs. Finally, after what seemed like an eternity, her body went limp. I held her for a few more seconds, then dropped her to the floor. I rushed into the kitchen, and wet a towel, soaking it with bleach and dish water, I washed all around her neck and poured bleach into her hair and mouth. I didn't know if any of my hair fibers fell on her, but the bleach would disintegrate the sweat and take the slight traces of DNA off of the hair if there was any left behind.

After I did the best I could, I wiped off everything

Hood Rich

I thought I touched and rushed out of that house, ran through the back yard, and jumped into the Buick, storming away from Tanya's crib. She was a dirty bitch. Had I not been on point, not only would I have been lying where School Boy and Lost Boy were, but she would have gotten a hefty lump sum for my murder. I had to get the fuck out of Chicago as soon as I could. My life depended on it.

***

Back at the safe house, I paced the floor, high as a kite. I was sleepy, but way too paranoid to allow my eyes to close. I thought there was somebody breaking in. My eyes would close, then I would jerk my head up and smack myself, going out of my mind waiting on Taylor to call me. I finally texted Yani, hoping she was awake. After waiting a few moments for her to respond to my messages, I decided to just call her, but she didn't pick up. I immediately started to worry about her overdosing on that heroin. Or worse, somebody kidnapping her.

I paced until about 8 o'clock the next morning. That was when the call from Taylor came through. "What took you so fucking long to get at me, Taylor, man? Damn."

"The world don't revolve around you, li'l nigga. I'm calling now. Chill out. Fuck, it's too early for this shit."

I took the phone off of my ear and mugged it. This nigga. Every time I had to interact with this clown, I wanted to kill him. I was feeling like that more than ever, especially after whacking Tanya.

"What's good, Taylor? Let's get this shit over with." I was trying to sound as calm as I could.

He yawned into the phone. "I been tracking him all night. Everything seems to be in place. I'm going to meet you at Bob's Used Car Lot. We'll discuss the details there." He yawned again. "Meet me there in a half an hour." The phone disconnected.

I mugged my phone again and put it back up. How the fuck was I supposed to get all the way over to Western? Did this idiot even think about that? I shook my head and exhaled. I had to shit so bad my lower back was hurting. I loaded up my bag of things and headed for the back door.

I exited the building and strode across the backyard and opened the gate. Stepping into the alley, I made my way down it toward the busy street, looking my shoulder every few steps I took. I knew I was in the heartland of the Four Corner Hustlers. I was praying I could make it to the El train station without running into any of my oppositions. The chance was slim, but it was all I could do.

I thought about calling Taylor's punk-ass back and telling him to come and pick me up. After all, he'd dropped me off there. But I decided against it. Maybe he had his reasons for not wanting us to be seen together in the daytime. But then, why would he be asking to meet me at the car lot? I was slightly confused.

I was halfway down the alley when a wino stumbled out of a garage, singing to himself. "You got a smile so bright. You know you should have been a candle. I'm holding you so tight. You know you should have been a handle." He spun in a circle with a brown paper bag in his hand that held a bottle of liquor. He smelled like piss and alcohol. The sugary kind, like Night Train or something like that. "Young Blood. Young Blood, ain't this how they do it? He broke into a crazy Temptation-like dance, wobbled his knees and hitting a half-split before popping back up and moonwalking. "Yeah, yeah, yeah."

The closer he got, the worse he smelled. I pinched my nose. "Man if you don't get yo' stanking ass away from me, I'ma put two holes in your chest and let yo' ass air out. Keep it moving, old head. Straight up." I pointed in his face. I wasn't playing with his old ass. My stomach was bubbling, and I wanted to body Pesos and get the fuck out of Chicago.

"Aw, muthafucka, you wanna hit people with garbage cans?" He backed up and turned his face into a snarl. "Well, come on, Cletus. Come on. It ain't but a short walk you gon' walk over, but you gon' limp back." He held up his guards. "Luke, I am your father."

I side-stepped him, grabbed the back of his head, and slung him into the garage, where he flew face-first into the door and fell on his ass. He sat there for a minute, shaking his head as if to clear it.

"Look, old man. Take yo' drunk ass home. I ain't got time for you right now. I gotta be on my way." I turned my back on him and proceeded to put a li'l pep in my step, looking over my shoulder at him.

He slowly got to his feet and cracked his neck, first to the right, and then to the left. "What is it good for? Huh! What is it good for? Absolutely nothing!

Aw!" He began runnin' in my direction again with his head down. This time I knew he was on bidness because he'd knocked over his cheap-ass wine. It spilled onto the ground of the alley. The brown paper bag was soaked. He hollered at the top of his lungs.

I was tired of this shit. I dropped my bag and threw up my guards. I waited for him to get within arm's reach before I pivoted and swung a left hook connecting with his jawbone, rocking his ass. My knuckle got to throbbing right away.

His head jerked to the side before he staggered on his feet and fell to both knees in the alley. "Ah, shit. Mama, he whooping my ass. He whooping my ass, Mama! Ah!" he screamed. "Well, you better get yo' ass up and keep fighting. This revolution will not be televised!" He jumped up and raised his right arm in the air. "Come on, freaky Jason. Come on. I ain't got time. You shouldn't've did that to Aretha."

I scrunched my face. I didn't know what the hell he was talkin' about. Who was Aretha? Who was Jason? "Look, old man, I gotta be on my way. I ain't tryna fight you no mo'. Now, git!" I stomped my foot at him as if he were a dog.

His eyes were open wide, bloodshot, yet they were seeing me. I could tell he was off his rocker. Blood oozed out of his mouth and dripped off his bottom lip. He hopped on one leg while he kept the Karate Kid pose. "Daniel-son! Daniel-son! Get 'im, Daniel-son." He hopped as close as he could and kicked his dirty work boots up, then fell away to the ground, busting his shit. I could smell the funk from his balls and ass. He needed to keep his legs down.

As soon as he hit the ground, he jumped back up.

"Say, man, let me borrow a couple of dollars until I get my check on the first. It's hard out here for a pimp. Hos ain't acting right." He popped his collar and held his hand out.

I smacked that muthafucka out of my face and punched him in the jaw, then gave him one hard upper cut that knocked his ass out cold. He flipped onto his chest and started snoring with blood running out of his mouth, his right leg twitching.

"Bitch-ass wine head. I don't know what you though this was." I picked up my bag and made my way out of that alley. I didn't make it more than ten feet when I heard a woman's voice.

"Oh my God, y'all, somebody done beat up Cube uncle. That dude just robbed him! Help! Help!" she screamed.

I looked around to see where the voice was coming from and located a heavyset sista with her head sticking out of the house's window. She put two fingers in her mouth and whistled.

My heart dropped. I took off running and made it out of the alley and onto the busy street. Once there, I looked both ways to see if there was a city transit bus coming, but saw nothing other than cars. Fuck. I was sick.

I looked over my shoulder and saw about ten dudes standing around Cube's uncle's body. One of was knelt down on one knee, trying to help him up. The other ones looked in my direction. A big, muscle-bound dude with a black beater on took a gun from out of his lower back and aimed at me. *Boo-wa. Boo-wa.* He took off running in my direction with the rest of his crew.

"Shit!" I ran into the busy street, waiting for six cars to pass by before I ran across it and took off running down Prairie with the heavy bag in my hand. When I got to the corner on 111th street, I ran onto the block and almost shit on myself when I saw it was packed with about fifty dudes. All of them were dressed in blue with blue rags around their necks.

I froze in place with my eyes bugged out of my head. I knew for a fact if they knew who I was, they wouldn't have hesitated to gun me down, so I took off running. Because I did, they started to murmur amongst themselves. Then I knew there was a group of them giving chase.

I was running as fast as I could. I could barely breathe. The shit in my gut and the drug usage had me winded, but I was still running stride-for-stride.

I ran back across the busy street when I heard two more shots ring out behind me. Then five shots. I knew they were busting at me. I was out of my mind with hysteria.

I took an alley, then ran along a gangway on 108th and Prairie. That let me back into another alley where there were about fifteen dudes in gold and black sitting alongside a garage. When they saw me approach, they jumped up and took their guns out. One of them yelled, "Hold it right there," with both of his guns aimed at me. He had five-point stars all over his face.

"Twelve coming. They just bent the corner! Get the of here!" I yelled, knowing it was all I could say to prevent being gunned down. A nigga could be caught running on nobody's block in Chicago if they didn't know who he was, or where he was coming from. Cats deemed everybody a threat. The only way a nigga could get around that is if he made it seem like the police were on bullshit. That was my only hope, so I just ran wit' it, praying silently in my head.

All of the dudes got to picking their money up off of the ground and running in different directions. The one who had his guns aimed at me put them away and took off running.

I breathed a sigh of relief and ran into the back of one of the houses and hid under the porch. My heart was pounding in my chest. I was worried out of my mind. I couldn't breathe, and to make matters ten times worse, I was next to a woman's dead body. The scent was so strong that I kept dry heaving.

I looked down on her and saw that her throat had been cut. Her face was bluish-brown and swollen. Her body was boated with a fizz spilling out of her belly button.

A bunch of voices came into the back yard. I could make out one more than the others. "Where that nigga go, Jo? He gotta be around here somewhere. Lord an' 'em said he ran in the alley talking about twelve," said the voice. "Any nigga find him, I got ten stacks on the fool," he hollered. "Damn, it stank back here!" he said, and then I could hear feet traipsing through the grass.

I scooted all the way back under the porch, and moved the woman's body to conceal me. When I rolled her over, rats began to scatter. There were worms, roaches, and maggots crawled all over her as well. I almost lost my mind and squealed at the top of my lungs. I scooted all the way back on my ass and slammed my head against the bottom of the porch. They ran all over my lap, screeching in their retreat.

Looking out, I could see the yard filling up with more and more dudes. They huddled up and pulled their guns out. It was freaking me out. I felt the rats crawling over me, along with various bugs. I knew if I moved in the slightest or made a noise that could potentially tip the dudes off, they would've murdered me for sure. I was stuck between a rock and a hard place. I didn't know what to do.

Suddenly, out of nowhere, gunfire erupted.

Hood Rich

Chapter 15

Boom. Boom. Boom. Boom. "Kill them niggas, Lord! Bust! Bust," one of the men yelled, and then there was a bunch of gunfire that ensued. I didn't know who they were bucking at or if the were in fact bucking at me, but I got as low as I could and covered my head while the bugs and rodents crawled all over me. I didn't understand what was going on until I made it through the gun battle and I was still not hit. I waited for two minutes after the shooting stopped to look out from under the porch. The yard was empty. I didn't know where everybody was, and I wasn't taking any chances. I crawled back under the porch and called, Taylor. His bitch-ass was going to have to come and get me. Forget that."

***

I slid into the back seat of his car thirty minutes later, fuming. "Man what the fuck took you so long?" I asked, shaking because I was so heated. It had started to rain. The sky was dark, and the rain was coming down like hail.

"You didn't know exactly where you were. I had to drive around this area until I was able to try and piece together what you were describing. Why do you smell so bad?" he asked, balling up his face. He looked like he was going to be sick.

"Man, I wish I could sit in front of a fan and force you to smell me. You had me under a fucking porch with a dead bitch, man. How else am I supposed to smell?"

Hood Rich

He opened his glove box and tossed me a bottle of Axe body spray. "Huh, put some of that on, or else I'ma throw up. You smell horrible, like ass and death."

I sprayed the Axe into the palm of my hand and rubbed my nose and around my nostrils so I could smell it. I didn't spray a lick on my body because I didn't care about his nose. I wish he would have puked. It would serve him right for taking so damn long. I tossed the bottle on the passenger seat.

"We're headed to Joliet, Illinois. That is where, Pesos is meeting up with Roman Velez this afternoon. I'm going to have you get to him first. Take care of your business and get all of the money he has with him. After you finish the job, I'm finished with you. A deal is a deal." He turned onto the expressway and picked up speed.

I sent Yani a text asking her if she was awake and okay. She'd not reached out to me all morning. I was becoming more and more worried. That was the only problem with loving somebody. If you did, you thought about and worried about them all day long like I did about her. I think having so many run-ins with death had me loving her more and more every single day.

"How do I know that after I handle this business for you, you won't still turn my ass in? I mean, what would stop you from doing so? I can already see you're a dirty-ass pig." I knew I shouldn't have been talking so reckless to him, but fuck, dude. One, he was a cop. And two, he was a bitch-nigga to me. I didn't like how he got down, and I knew he had something rotten up his sleeve. I just didn't know what it was, but I was worried, to say the least.

"That's the thing, you don't know what I'm gon' do. You can only roll wit' the punches and find out the ending later," he laughed. "Wit' yo' tough-ass." He stepped on the gas.

I sat back in my seat with a mug on my face. I couldn't figure this pig out. I didn't understand why he needed me to kill Pesos. He could have easily hit him up and covered up the murder. Cops in Chicago were known for doing exactly that. I knew there was something more at play here that I was missing. I felt weird. I just couldn't quite put my finger on it. "Say, Taylor, what's yo' deal, Jo?"

"The deal is you kill him and give me the money. That's my deal. I thought that was already clear." He adjusted his rearview mirror and we locked eyes.

"Man, you know what the fuck I mean. I mean why do you need me to kill Pesos so bad? Why you can't do it? I know you got that killer shit in you, especially when it comes to killing us black niggas in the hood. So, what gives?"

He switched lanes and sped past a rusty old pick-up truck that had a bunch of smoke billowing out of its pipes. "I leave that hood shit to you hood niggas. It ain't my place to clean up y'all messes. If you start a fire, you should put it out. It's as simple as that. I'm trying to stay right with the Lord above."

I almost punched him in the back of his head. "You got to be fucking kidding me. So you won't kill one of us, but you'll let us kill each other and take the money, huh? Well, ain't you just a saint?" I rolled my eyes and scoffed at his ass.

"Hey, it is what it is. You live your life, and I'll

live mine. I'm 50 years old. Twice your age. Let's see you get there."

"I don't care how old you are, homie. Just hold up your end of the deal. After I do all that crap, let me live my life. Let me put this behind me. I swear, you'll never have to worry about me stepping foot in your city again."

He laughed and nodded his head. "Man, Jahrome, that is probably the most honest thing I've ever heard from yo' mouth. I know for a fact you'll never step again, so I'll take your word for at least that." He shook his head and turned on an Isley Brothers track.

I sat back and tried texting Yani again. *What is going on with my baby?* I wondered.

***

We arrived in Joliet about thirty minutes later, and ten minutes after that Taylor pulled into the alley behind a red-bricked duplex that had a black and blue Rolls Royce parked in back of it. The neighborhood looked as if it was inhabited by middle-class people. All of the houses looked nice. Their lawns were mowed. There was no litter on the steers for as far as I could see. All of the cars in the driveways looked more new than old. I was sure this hood was full of white people.

Taylor turned around in his seat as the rain beat off of his windshield. "Look, like I said, I been tracking Pesos. It's gon' be him and one other dude in the house. The dude works as his bodyguard. I don't know how you're going to handle him, but that's up to you. There is five million dollars in cash inside of the house that Pesos will be looking to hand over to Roman Velez for his security, and a large quantity of tar heroin that's being shipped from El Salvador. The money is mine. Pesos' heroin is both yours and mine. Do what you gotta do and get this over with. I'll be sitting right here and waiting for you to come out with my money. You dig that?" He dug into his shirt pocket. "This is for you." He handed me a chrome silencer for my Glock. "I know you can use this," he smiled.

I took it from him and pulled my Glock out, then screwed the silencer inside of it, making sure it was tight. I took my second Glock .40 and put it in the small of my back. "I'll be back in ten minutes. Be ready to move this whip at that time." I pulled my hood over my head and stepped out into the pouring rain with a mug on my face. I was worried about Yani and ready to get this shit over with. Nall, I didn't trust Taylor, but it's like what other choice did I have to get this stankin'-ass pig off of my back? I couldn't think of any.

I made my way around the side of the house, and onto the porch. It was raining so bad that it was pitch black outside, and it was only about twelve o'clock in the afternoon. I looked both ways down each side of the street. The wind blew rain into my face and splashed me something good. I passed gas to let some of the pressure from my stomach. I could feel a turd sitting right there in my butt. I needed to shit bad. I took a deep breath and rang the doorbell to the residence, took the Glock out of my waistband, and cocked it. I could hear the sound of heavy footsteps on the other side of the door.

"Who is it?" came a deep voice.

"It's Mike. Hey, man, I need to use your phone. My car stalled out on me about a block up the road. I'm stranded. You think you can help me out?" I asked, trying to sound as proper as I possibly could. I looked both ways again.

"Nall, man, you can't use our phone, homeboy. Go ask the neighbors or something. G'on, get the fuck off of my porch."

I lowered my head as I felt my heart begin to race. I felt that murderous feeling. I could taste salt in my mouth. I clenched my teeth. "But I really need to use your phone. I have my daughter in the car. She's only two years old. Why don't you have some freaking compassion, asshole." I kicked the door and acted like I was about to walk off of the porch. I started talking to myself, mumbling under my breath, but it was all an act. I knew muthafuckas in Chicago hated when a nigga kicked their door. It was enough to get a nigga killed.

I heard the locks turning on the door, and then it I flew open. "Listen here, you punk muthafucka. I know you didn't just kick my door like you done lost your fucking –"

I spun on my toes, upped my .40, and let it spit. *Whoosh. Whoosh. Whoosh. Whoosh.* The bullets slammed into his face, ripping it apart. His brains were smacked out of the back of his head and spilled down his neck. He fell in the doorway, collapsing sideways. I rolled his big bitch-ass back into the house and stepped over him, closing the door lightly. I could hear the television. It sounded like somebody was watching a basketball game. The squeaking of the hardwood floors was apparent.

I held the gun out in front of me, tip-toeing through the house. In the living room, I saw a television hanging on the wall. The fireplace was lit and roaring. The carpet felt soft under my Airmax 9011. I heard the clinking of a plate and smelled chicken. My stomach growled.

"Say, folk, who was that at the door, G," came Pesos' voice. I knew it as soon as I heard it. I'd never forget it. It was the last voice my father heard before he was killed by him.

"Hey, G. What the fuck going on up there?" he hollered.

I rushed into the dining room and drew both Glocks on his bitch-ass. Pesos was sitting in front of a table full of food with a napkin around his neck, acting as a bib. When he looked up and saw me, his eyes got big and he slammed both hands down on the table. "Ain't this a bitch?" he mugged me.

"Yeah, fuck-nigga. It's a bitch on her period. Put yo' muthafucking hands up right now." I cocked the hammer of the Glock in my left hand. Under my mask, my face was turned into a scowl. I was envisioning the scene when Pesos had gunned down my father in front of me before hitting me up. That made me emotional and angry. "Put yo hands up, bitch-nigga!"

"Man, fuck you, nigga! Make me put my hands up," he snarled.

Whoosh. Whoosh. Two bullets, one in each shoulder. I knocked him out of his seat and flung him into the wall. He must've tried to hang onto the tablecloth because he wound up spilling all of the food down with him. It landed on top of his body as he writhed in pain.

"Aw, you bitch-ass nigga. You shot a King, nigga. You just shot a muthafucking Boss." He struggled to stand up, his bloody hand smearing plasma all over the wall.

I took my mask off. "Yeah, bitch-nigga. Karma is a muthafucka, ain't it," I said, exposing my face. I wanted him to know who I was before I killed him. The rules of the slums said a nigga was always supposed to look his enemy in the eyes before he killed him. I wanted to do more than that. I wanted the nigga to take a picture of my face all the way to hell where he belonged.

It took him a while to register who I was, but I could tell when he did because his eyes lit up and his mouth opened. "Aye, fuck, nigga, you still alive?"

I aimed both guns at him with my fingers on the triggers. "Yeah, nigga, but you ain't." I lowered my eyes and tightened my fingers on the triggers.

"Wait, Jahrome! The money! Get the money first!" Taylor said, running in from the front of the house. He rushed over to me and stood in front of me, blocking my line of fire.

I backed away with my eyes locked in on Pesos. I didn't give a fuck what took place, I was killing his bitch-ass before it was all said and done with.

"Pops? What the fuck? This how you getting down on me?" He asked, looking up at Taylor. Blood pouring out of the holes in his shoulders. He squinted his eyes and winced in pain.

"Just tell him where the money is, Pesos. Ain't

no reason to die for it. He already knows it's here."
He tried to get Pesos to stand. "Come on?"

I aimed both of my guns at them again. "Why the fuck is he calling you his Pops? I thought Shorty Freeman was yo' Pops."

"Boy, put them guns down. You can't kill him or we'll never get the money," Taylor said, sitting Pesos into a chair.

Pesos staggered against him with blood saturating his clothes. He held his arms tight to his body, his face screwed into a ball of pain. He tried to push Taylor away. "Get the fuck off of me, you snake-ass nigga. How the fuck you gon' marry my mother and do me like this?" he snapped with spit flying out of his mouth.

Taylor backed up and took out his service weapon. "Don't bring my wife into this. You decided that you wanted to be in these streets. Well, this is what's happening. Where is the money?" Sweat ran down the side of his black face. His eyes were open wide.

"Fuck you! I should have never trusted yo' ass. I should've murdered you as soon as my mother told me she was marrying yo' cop-ass. We don't fuck wit' pork in my family." He looked as if he was in a frenzy.

Taylor curled his lip. "Pesos, come on, man. Don't make me do this shit to you. I swore to your mother I was going to keep you safe. That I wouldn't lay a hand on you even though I know what you're doing out here in these streets, but you're making it awfully hard. Now, give up the fucking money or I'ma have to let Heinous there fuck you up. It's either/or." Taylor took another step back and frowned. "Give it up!"

Pesos held his right shoulder. Blood gushed through his fingers. "Nigga, bury me a muthafuckin' G! I ain't givin' you or this bitch-nigga shit! A pussy die a million deaths. A nigga like me will only die once." He spit a yellow loogie onto Taylor's chest.

I scrunched up my face at the sight of it. That shit looked so gross. Taylor looked down at the spit and gagged, jerked back, and smacked the shit out of him so hard he knocked him to the floor and out cold. Pesos' mouth was open wide, his eyes closed. I could see spurts of blood trickling out of his shoulder wounds. It formed a puddle around his body.

"That's yo' muthafuckin' son? Are you kidding me, Taylor?" I snapped, not knowing what to do. If this muthafucka would do this shit to his own kid, I could only imagine what he had in store for me. This punk couldn't be trusted as far as I could throw his big ass. I needed to find a way to wiggle out of this situation.

"That's my step-son, and none of this is personal. It's just business. I gotta have that money, and I gotta have it right now." He knelt on one knee and smacked Pesos across the face, jarring him awake. "Get yo' li'l ass up and take me to the money. I'm not gon' ask you again!" he snapped, grabbing him by the collar of his shirt.

Pesos gagged and tried to stop the shirt from cutting off his air circulation. Blood dripped down the length of his forearm and dripped off of his elbow. "Ack. Ack. I can't. You bitch-ass nigga," he started before Taylor slapped him in the mouth again, busting it.

Taylor picked him up and slammed the gun to his temple. "You see, what you li'l niggas fail to understand is I used to be in the streets just like you two are. Y'all ain't showing me nothing new. You li'l punks are just more stupid. You don't think before you make moves. You're impulsive." He put his forearm under his neck. "Where is the money? Tell me right the fuck now or take one to the gut. You got three seconds. One. Two."

Pesos struggled under his forearm. He gagged, and I could tell he was trying to let Taylor know he was ready to talk.

"Aw, you ready to give it up? Huh? Well, just to make sure." He put the barrel of his gun to Pesos' knee and pulled the trigger. *Whoosh!* Fire spit from the barrel. A shell popped out of the gun and hit the wall.

Pesos fell to the carpet, wincing in pain. "You Uncle Tom son of a bitch! Aw, shit. You done blew my knee off. You done blew off my muthafucking knee. Lord have mercy, this hurt. Aw, my God!"

He rolled around on the carpet in a bloody mess. I couldn't help laughing at his bitch-ass. There was the fact I didn't like this chump at all. The more pain he had to go through before I ended his life with a slug made me more and more happy. I felt like he was getting everything he deserved. I couldn't wait to finish him off.

Taylor knelt and grabbed a handful of his shirt, placing the gun to his neck. "Where is the money?"

Pesos squeezed his eyelids together and started to cough, shaking on the carpet as if he was freezing.

"It's in the washing machine downstairs. In a black garbage bag. Take it. Get the fuck out of here. Please. Fuck that money." He lay back on the carpet and placed his forearm over his eyes. "This shit hurt!"

Taylor yanked him up by the throat. "Get yo' punk-ass up. You finna take me to this money." He dragged him through the living room and to the back door of the house. "Open the door for me, Heinous. Once we get this money, we can part ways. I got what I wanted. Your slate is clean wit' me. That's my word."

I opened the door and held it wide. "That sound good to me." Though it's what I told him, I knew I wasn't about to leave that house without putting slugs all up in his ass. I still couldn't get over the fact he was doing his son like this. I could only imagine what he had in store for me. I know I kept saying that, but it was just a fact.

He threw Pesos down the back steps. He rolled all the way down them and wound up on his back in the basement. Taylor jumped off the last three steps to land beside Pesos. He grabbed his shirt and dragged him over to the washing machine. Once there, he laid him on the floor and kicked him in the stomach.

"You ain't so muthafucking tough after all, you li'l bitch. It better be in here, too." Taylor snapped and placed his gun back into his holster, leaned over, and opened the washing machine's door. He stuck his hand inside of it and pulled out a black garbage bag, setting it on the floor. He knelt beside it and opened the bag. His eyes got big as silver dollars. "Aw, now this what I'm talking about." He nodded his head, excited, stuck his hand back into the washing machine, and pulled out another bag just as big as the first one. He opened it and went through it, giving Pesos no mind.

Pesos used the distraction to slide his hand between the side of the washing machine and the dryer. I watched him from start to finish. When his hand came from behind it, it was holding a .38 Special handgun. He cocked the hammer and aimed it at Taylor. "You dirty muthafucka! I should've done this a long time ago!"

Taylor popped his head up from the bag and looked down on him. When he saw the gun in his hand, he stood stupidly and went for the gun in his holster.

Boom. Boom. Boom.. Six shots from Pesos' revolver slammed into the detective.

He aimed his gun at the man on the floor and pulled his trigger. *Whoosh. Whoosh.* The bullets spit out of the silenced weapon, rocking Pesos on the floor. Two headshots. His brains splattered outside of his skull. The entire basement was filled with smoke and the scent of hot gunpowder. Taylor fell on his back with his eyes opened wide. He stuck two fingers into one of the bullet holes in his chest, looked at it, and saw the blood. Then his eyes crossed and closed.

I rushed over and grabbed the bag of money. Looked down into it, I confirmed it was filled with bundles and bundles of cash. Definitely more than enough money to start a new life with Yani. I had to get to my baby. Had to get to her and leave this side of the country.

I tied both of the garbage bags into a knot and lowered myself to one knee to get the car keys from Taylor. He was laid out on his back with his eyes closed. I slid my hand around his waist and into his right front pocket. Time was of the essence. I needed to get the hell out of there, and fast. Gunshots fired in an all-white neighborhood meant the police would be reacting in a matter of minutes.

My hand slid into the pocket, and just as my fingers touched the keys, Taylor grabbed my wrist and held onto it.

"Argh! Argh! Help me, Jahrome! Get me out of here and to a hospital. I'll make all of your troubles disappear," he pleaded.

I cracked him in the jaw with my elbow. "Get the fuck off of me, pig! You wasn't leaving this house, no way. You dirty son of a bitch." I aimed my Glock down at him. "Rest in peace!"

"My partner got all of the footage on you. You pull that trigger and you're through. I'm the only one that can clear it out. Don't do this." He coughed up a glob of blood and fell backward.

"Your partner? Who the fuck is he?" I asked with my mind racing. Now there was somebody else who had all of the goods on me? I was sick. I was sure I would have been able to start over fresh once Taylor was dead. "What the fuck you mean, Taylor?" I pressed the barrel to his forehead.

His eyes closed, and then his face turned sideways. "You thought I was stupid." He started to cough. "I'm not stupid, Jahrome. Save my life or lose yours. I mean that. Pull that trigger and your life will never be the same."

I felt a chill go down my spine. Before I could think logically, I pulled the trigger one time, splashing his brains. "Fuck you! It is what it is."

I grabbed the keys out of his pocket, the bags of money, and then broke out of the back door, jumping into his whip. I had to get to Yani. We needed to get the fuck out of Illinois.

I drove his car about twenty blocks away and stole a red Chevy Prism. I drove that one fifteen miles and traded it in for a Jeep Grand Cherokee. I jumped on the highway, storming my way to Yani.

My heart pounding in my chest, I drove with my left hand and texted her with my right, telling her I was on my way and to be ready. That I missed her. My throat felt tight. I couldn't wait to see my woman. I honestly needed her after all I'd been through. Multiple dead bodies flashed through my head over and over again. They showed up so much that I felt like I was going crazy. I needed to be around Yani. I needed her to heal me. I was feeling so sick.

We had five million dollars. Five million plus all of the cash she had with her. We were sure to be able to live a good life. A life on the run, but a good one, nonetheless.

Damn, I was fien'ing for her like never before. I was only thirty minutes away from my queen. My head began to spin as one murder after the next began to play through it again. There was the sound of a chalkboard being scratched in my ears. I felt my heart pounding, and I still had to shit like crazy.

Somehow, by the grace of God, I was able to make it back to our hotel in one piece. I jumped out of the Jeep, grabbed both bags of money, and made my way inside of the hotel, taking my keycard out in the elevator. I wanted to see my baby so bad. I needed her.

When the elevator dinged, the doors opened and I rushed down the hallway and to our room door. I nearly dropped the card twice trying to fit it into the lock. When it turned green, I took a deep breath in anticipation of seeing my woman.

The door swung in and I stepped inside of the room. I was hit by a strong stench that nearly caused me to vomit. I looked forward and dropped both bags onto the floor. What I saw took the breath right out of my body. I fell to my knees because I couldn't take it anymore.

"Yani! No!"

To Be Continued...
KingPin Killaz 3
Coming Soon

Kingpin Killaz 2

Submission Guideline

Submit the first three chapters of your completed manuscript to ldpsubmissions@gmail.com, subject line: Your book's title. The manuscript must be in a .doc file and sent as an attachment. Document should be in Times New Roman, double spaced and in size 12 font. Also, provide your synopsis and full contact information. If sending multiple submissions, they must each be in a separate email.

Have a story but no way to send it electronically? You can still submit to LDP/Ca$h Presents. Send in the first three chapters, written or typed, of your completed manuscript to:

LDP: Submissions Dept
Po Box 870494
Mesquite, Tx 75187

DO NOT send original manuscript. Must be a duplicate.

Provide your synopsis and a cover letter containing your full contact information.

Thanks for considering LDP and Ca$h Presents.

Hood Rich

BOW DOWN TO MY GANGSTA

By **Ca$h**

TORN BETWEEN TWO

By **Coffee**

BLOOD STAINS OF A SHOTTA **III**

By **Jamaica**

STEADY MOBBIN **III**

By **Marcellus Allen**

BLOOD OF A BOSS **V**

By **Askari**

LOYAL TO THE GAME **IV**

LIFE OF SIN II

By **T.J. & Jelissa**

A DOPEBOY'S PRAYER **II**

By **Eddie "Wolf" Lee**

IF LOVING YOU IS WRONG... **III**

LOVE ME EVEN WHEN IT HURTS **II**

By **Jelissa**

TRUE SAVAGE **VI**

By **Chris Green**

BLAST FOR ME **III**

A BRONX TALE

DUFFLE BAG CARTEL

By **Ghost**

ADDICTIED TO THE DRAMA **III**

Kingpin Killaz 2

By **Jamila Mathis**
LIPSTICK KILLAH **III**
CRIME OF PASSION **II**
By **Mimi**
WHAT BAD BITCHES DO **III**
KILL ZONE **II**
By **Aryanna**
THE COST OF LOYALTY **II**
By **Kweli**
SHE FELL IN LOVE WITH A REAL ONE **II**
By **Tamara Butler**
LOVE SHOULDN'T HURT **III**
RENEGADE BOYS **III**
By **Meesha**
CORRUPTED BY A GANGSTA **IV**
By **Destiny Skai**
A GANGSTER'S CODE **III**
By **J-Blunt**
KING OF NEW YORK III
By **T.J. Edwards**
GORILLAS IN THE BAY II
De'Kari
THE STREETS ARE CALLING II
Duquie Wilson
KINGPIN KILLAZ III
Hood Rich
STEADY MOBBIN' **III**

Hood Rich

Marcellus Allen

SINS OF A HUSTLA II

ASAD

HER MAN, MINE'S TOO **II**

CASH MONEY HOES

Nicole Goosby

TRIGGADALE II

Elijah R. Freeman

<u>Available Now</u>

<u>RESTRAINING ORDER **I & II**</u>

By **CA$H & Coffee**

<u>LOVE KNOWS NO BOUNDARIES **I II & III**</u>

By **Coffee**

<u>RAISED AS A GOON I, II, III & IV</u>

<u>BRED BY THE SLUMS I, II, III</u>

<u>BLAST FOR ME I & II</u>

<u>ROTTEN TO THE CORE I III</u>

By **Ghost**

<u>LAY IT DOWN **I & II**</u>

<u>LAST OF A DYING BREED</u>

<u>BLOOD STAINS OF A SHOTTA I & II</u>

By **Jamaica**

<u>LOYAL TO THE GAME</u>

<u>LOYAL TO THE GAME II</u>

<u>LOYAL TO THE GAME III</u>

Kingpin Killaz 2

LIFE OF SIN

By **TJ & Jelissa**

BLOODY COMMAS I & II

SKI MASK CARTEL I II & III

KING OF NEW YORK I II

By **T.J. Edwards**

IF LOVING HIM IS WRONG…I & II

LOVE ME EVEN WHEN IT HURTS

By **Jelissa**

WHEN THE STREETS CLAP BACK I & II III

By **Jibril Williams**

A DISTINGUISHED THUG STOLE MY HEART I II & III

LOVE SHOULDN'T HURT I II

RENEGADE BOYS I & II

By **Meesha**

A GANGSTER'S CODE I & II

By **J-Blunt**

PUSH IT TO THE LIMIT

By **Bre' Hayes**

BLOOD OF A BOSS **I, II, III & IV**

By **Askari**

THE STREETS BLEED MURDER **I, II & III**

THE HEART OF A GANGSTA I II& III

By **Jerry Jackson**

CUM FOR ME

CUM FOR ME 2

CUM FOR ME 3

Hood Rich

Kingpin Killaz 2

TRUE SAVAGE **V**

By **Chris Green**

A DOPEBOY'S PRAYER

By **Eddie "Wolf" Lee**

THE KING CARTEL **I, II & III**

By **Frank Gresham**

THESE NIGGAS AIN'T LOYAL **I, II & III**

By **Nikki Tee**

GANGSTA SHYT **I II &III**

By **CATO**

THE ULTIMATE BETRAYAL

By **Phoenix**

BOSS'N UP **I , II & III**

By **Royal Nicole**

I LOVE YOU TO DEATH

By Destiny J

I RIDE FOR MY HITTA

I STILL RIDE FOR MY HITTA

By **Misty Holt**

LOVE & CHASIN' PAPER

By **Qay Crockett**

TO DIE IN VAIN

SINS OF A HUSTLA

By **ASAD**

BROOKLYN HUSTLAZ

By **Boogsy Morina**

BROOKLYN ON LOCK I & II

Hood Rich

By **Sonovia**

GANGSTA CITY

By **Teddy Duke**

A DRUG KING AND HIS DIAMOND I & II III

A DOPEMAN'S RICHES

HER MAN, MINE'S TOO

By **Nicole Goosby**

TRAPHOUSE KING **I II & III**

KINGPIN KILLAZ

By **Hood Rich**

LIPSTICK KILLAH **I, II**

CRIME OF PASSION

By **Mimi**

STEADY MOBBN' **I, II**

By **Marcellus Allen**

WHO SHOT YA **I, II**

Renta

GORILLAZ IN THE BAY

DE'KARI

TRIGGADALE

Elijah R. Freeman

GOD BLESS THE TRAPPERS I, II, III

THESE SCANDALOUS STREETS I, II, III

FEAR MY GANGSTA I, II, III

THESE STREETS DON'T LOVE NOBODY I, II

Tranay Adams

THE STREETS ARE CALLING

Kingpin Killaz 2

Duquie Wilson

Hood Rich

BOOKS BY LDP'S CEO, CA$H

TRUST IN NO MAN

TRUST IN NO MAN 2

TRUST IN NO MAN 3

BONDED BY BLOOD

SHORTY GOT A THUG

THUGS CRY

THUGS CRY 2

THUGS CRY 3

TRUST NO BITCH

TRUST NO BITCH 2

TRUST NO BITCH 3

TIL MY CASKET DROPS

RESTRAINING ORDER

RESTRAINING ORDER 2

IN LOVE WITH A CONVICT

Coming Soon

BONDED BY BLOOD 2

BOW DOWN TO MY GANGSTA

Kingpin Killaz 2

www.ingramcontent.com/pod-product-compliance
Lightning Source LLC
Chambersburg PA
CBHW070022260626
47159CB00005B/1918